C000133642

A LAYER OF LOVE

A RECIPE FOR LOVE NOVEL

KELLY COLLINS

BOOK NOOK PRESS

Copyright © 2022 by Kelly Collins

All rights reserved.

No part of this book may be reproduced in any form or by any electronic or mechanical means, including information storage and retrieval systems, without written permission from the author, except for the use of brief quotations in a book review.

Cover by Graphics by Stacy

CHAPTER ONE

Recipes for Love. Courtney Sweet pushed the cookbook across the kitchen island. She had no idea where it came from. All she knew was it somehow found its way into her backpack.

If only it were that easy and there was a recipe. She'd make a fortune selling it.

She laughed all the way to her early riser's exercise group. This was her first meeting, and she hoped to make a few friends and talk about something other than action figures and anime.

Her son Jesse was entertaining, but nothing took the place of a bona fide friend. As for love ... that left the day Marcus did. She said three words that made him run. "Hey, I'm pregnant." That was almost eleven years ago, and she'd been single ever since.

Seeing her brother find happiness with Chloe only made her realize how much she needed the company of others. Why not add people with fitness? If it all worked out the way she hoped, she'd gain a few friends and lose a few pounds. Win-win.

She pulled into the parking lot of Pioneer Park, where several people in various athletic outfits milled about. It was an Aspen crowd dressed in designer duds who looked more like they were walking the runway than the nearby trail.

Courtney stared at her baggy, paint-splotched sweats, and the sneakers she hadn't worn in at least a year. She wasn't Aspen chic but Timberline real. She didn't get her hair cut in salons called Posh, but in front of her bathroom mirror with scissors dulled by her son's school projects.

She gave the crowd another glance and almost started her car to drive away, but a man hanging off to the side caught her attention. He wore baggy sweats like hers and a vintage Queen T-shirt. At least he had good taste in music.

She got out of her beat-up Jeep and made her way toward him, but it appeared the housewives of 81611 had the same idea and swooped in like crows attacking roadkill.

They lobbed questions at him like they were tossing hand grenades, and he avoided their interrogation like a professional landmine sweeper.

"Good morning," the group leader said in a high-pitched voice. She could have been an advertisement for Lululemon in her multi-colored ensemble. "This is a walking group that meets Monday, Wednesday, and Friday at this location. We'll do the four-mile path today. If you need a more intensive workout, consider adding weights." The woman bounced in place like she'd had one too many espressos. "Hopefully, you got to introduce yourselves, but if not, there's plenty of time during the trek. Shall we go?"

She led the way down the paved path. No one followed her initially. Courtney thought they were all waiting for the hot Omega man to go ahead of them. When he didn't budge, his fan-club trio walked on.

Once they were on the trail, Mr. Handsome followed. Maybe he was an ass man and liked the back-end view of things.

As she fell into line behind him, she appreciated the scenery he offered. Though his sweats were loose, they draped like a beautiful fondant frosting across his backside.

For that first mile, she hung back and took in the sights. The mountains and forest were lovely too.

Reminding herself that she joined the group to meet people, she double-timed her pace to catch up to him.

"Hey, how's it going?" she asked as she came upon his right.

He gave her a cursory glance followed by a frown. "Fine."

She laughed. "You know, when a woman says fine, it's anything but."

His scowl deepened, creating a deep furrow between his brows. He picked up his pace as if to escape her.

She resorted to a half walk and half jog, to keep up with him.

"Well, obviously, you're sight-impaired or gender challenged because I'm not a woman. I'm a man, and when we say fine, it's generally the truth."

"Fine."

He cocked his head and stared. "Is that anything but fine?"

She didn't know what his problem was. All she tried to be was friendly. "It's 'you're an idiot' fine."

He narrowed his eyes and seemed to lurch forward. When she looked down, she noticed his shoe was untied.

"You want me to teach you how to double knot?" she asked.

"Now, who's being a jerk?"

Her six-year-old inner child was fighting to be freed. All she wanted to do was stick her tongue out and possibly her foot to see him face plant on the pavement, but she reeled her unhappy woman-child in. "You're right. I apologize." The words had a bitter tang to them. It was fine to say sorry when she was in the wrong, but this guy was out of line.

"Look, I get it. You show up and think, I'll give the only guy in the group a go, but honestly, I'm not interested."

She nearly tripped over her shoes, and they were tied. Double knotted, in fact.

"You think I was trying to pick you up? Listen, dude, you're not my type."

He stopped and tied his shoe, and like an idiot, she waited for him. That was part of her problem. She was too accommodating ... well, she used to be, but that was nearly eleven years ago. Now she was simply afraid of putting herself out there. And just her luck, the first guy she strikes up a conversation with is a total troglodyte.

"Oh, you have a type?"

Her blood heated, and the pressure inside her built until her scalp itched. Having a conversation with this man was like sparring with a toad, warts, and all.

"Yes, I prefer them human with a smidge of decency, an ounce of kindness, and a spoonful of humility. What you are is a pound of pain in my ass."

"That's quite a recipe you've got going there. If I had to build one for myself, I'd want an hour of silence and a mile of space. If you added in a cool breeze, I'd be golden."

She snapped her fingers. "Wish granted." She marched a few feet ahead and took up residence between the group of women she'd never fit in with and the man who she never wanted to see again.

Fifteen minutes later, a phone rang, and she turned to see the guy stop to answer it. He let out a few expletives and left the group, jogging toward where they started.

The women in front talked about Dysport and Sculptra and who in town gave the best colonic. Courtney wondered how she'd gracefully bow out. Could she fake a turned ankle and hobble back to her car?

Her phone rang, and she breathed a sigh of relief when she stopped to answer it, and no one waited for her.

"Hello."

"Ms. Sweet. This is Abby, the nurse at Pine Elementary School."

Courtney's heart thundered in her chest. The nurse only called when something was wrong.

"Is Jesse okay?"

She picked up her pace until she was jogging to her car.

"Yes, he's fine, but Principal Cain asked me to call. She'd like you to come in. There was an event involving Jesse, and your presence is required."

What the hell was an event?

"Do I need to bring him a change of clothes?" The only thing she could come up with was an "accident," and Jesse hadn't wet his pants since he was three. There was the time Gage pinned him down and tickled him when he was six, but in her son's defense, he literally had nowhere else to go when his uncle wouldn't let him loose.

"No." She paused for a moment. "It's not that. Are you on your way?"

"He's not hurt?"

"No, but he's in trouble. There was a fight of sorts."

She swallowed and let the thought nearly choke her. Jesse wasn't the kind of kid who got into trouble.

"I'm on my way." She hung up and ran the rest of the way to her SUV. Whatever happened, there had to be a logical excuse.

Like a bat flying straight out of hell, she raced to the school and parked illegally in the staff parking lot. She opened the door and tried to exit, but the seatbelt choked her, so she sat back and took a few breaths. A calm, cool, and collected parent would take a moment to regroup and gain her bearings, but she was already wound up by Mr. Mean.

She yanked and tugged herself free and stomped toward the

front office. Jesse Sweet was exactly as his name described. He was sweet and kind and considerate. If there was a fight, he was the victim.

At the front office, she waited for the woman behind the desk to notice her. When she didn't, Courtney cleared her throat and tapped her nails on the counter to gain her attention.

The gray-haired woman looked up and pushed back the glasses perched precariously on the tip of her nose.

"Can I help you?"

"Sweet."

The older woman smiled. "Only on Mondays. By Friday, I'm an out-and-out ogre."

Courtney let out a frustrated sigh. "No, I'm Courtney Sweet, and I've been summoned here about my son, Jesse."

"Right." The woman whose nameplate read Mrs. Wheatley shook her head. "Principal Cain is waiting for you." She pointed down the hallway. "Last door. Knock before entering."

Courtney traveled the long corridor like she was walking the green mile. Each step that she grew closer to the door, the more her panic set in.

She'd always heard that being sent to the principal's office was like being sent to the firing squad, but she considered that the opinion of a ten-year-old in trouble. Everything was a life-or-death matter at that age, but she truly felt like she was approaching her demise.

Was it because Jesse was in trouble, and this might be the end of the sweet boy she knew and loved, and the start of him being a pre-teen? She shuddered to think about what that meant.

At the door, she raised her hand and let it fall to her side twice before she got the courage to follow through and knock. A shudder passed through her. What would be waiting when the principal told her to come inside?

She tapped the door four times. Four was always her lucky number, and she hoped it would hold.

"Come in," the firm voice called from the other side.

She gripped the handle and pushed the heavy door open.

Her jaw dropped when she saw who was waiting on the other side.

"You've got to be kidding me," Mr. Mean said.

Sitting beside him was a toothless little girl with brown curls and swollen lips.

On the other side of the room was an unhappy-looking but seemingly unscathed Jesse.

At her throne was Principal Cain.

All four of them stared at her.

Nope, four was no longer her lucky number.

CHAPTER TWO

"Unbelievable," Richard said, looking at the woman he'd met at the park. "What are the odds?"

She cocked her head to the side and stared into space. "There are too many variables to calculate, but I'd say they're pretty good since we're here."

Principal Cain asked the woman to come inside and close the door behind her.

"I'm assuming you two know each other?" she asked.

He snorted. "Know?" He shook his head. "Never met her."

The woman scowled at him before moving toward her son and squatting in front of the boy. He had to admit that hiding behind those baggy sweatpants was exactly what he appreciated—curves. He liked a woman with meat on her bones, but this woman would never be his. She was shrew-like—totally not his type.

He chuckled at the thought of having a type. He hadn't been with a woman since his wife died two years ago. It seemed like yesterday when he held her hand in the hospital. She lay lifeless and hooked to machines, but he was torn between wanting her to be okay and wanting to choke the life out of her. In the end, he didn't have a choice. She succumbed to the injuries she sustained in the car accident.

"Do you find this funny?" Principal Cain asked.

He shook his head. "Me? No, of course not." He pointed to his daughter, whose lip continued to swell despite the ice she kept putting on it. "Avery is missing her front teeth. That's not a laughing matter."

He heard the woman speaking softly to her son; she had a voice that would soothe a savage beast. She obviously only used that tone for special people. As soon as she was finished talking, she stood.

"From what I can gather, Avery picked up a rock first and lobbed it at Jesse." She settled her fists on her hips. "He was simply defending himself."

He pointed at her. "Listen, whatever your name is, that's not true." He turned to look at his daughter, who hung her head. She always did that when she was hiding something. "Okay, it might be true, but look at her." He reached over and tipped her head back. "Those were permanent teeth, and they need to be replaced." He would have rushed Avery and the teeth to a dentist if he had the teeth in hand. Rumor had it you could put them back in the sockets and secure them. Sometimes they reattached, but the nurse said the shattered teeth weren't salvageable.

Principal Cain slapped the desk and a cracking sound reverberated through the office. It sounded so much like thunder that he looked to the ceiling to make sure it wouldn't rain.

"I don't tolerate misbehavior in my office." Principal Cain glared at the woman. "Ms. Sweet, take a seat."

"Sweet?" He staunched the desire to roll his eyes. "Hardly."

"Enough," the principal yelled.

The Sweet woman raised her hand. "May I say something?"

"Do you have nice words?" the authoritarian asked.

The Sweet woman smiled. "I believe that all words can be nice words. It's how you use them that matters. For example, I can say, 'I hate that,' but it's all in context. What am I talking about?" She looked at Avery. "I hate that. The *that* means I hate that her front teeth are gone. But if I didn't explain, then you might have thought I meant the girl." She shook her head. "Sweetie, I don't hate you. I don't even know you. So, you see, words are all nice unless they are used in a negative way."

"Like when she called me a butthole and threw the rock." Jesse stuck his tongue out at Avery. "You throw like a girl."

Avery crossed her arms over her chest. "I am a girl."

"Avery," he said in a low warning tone. "We'll talk about this later. Right now, we need to pay attention to your principal."

"Since you haven't been formally introduced." Principal Cain looked at him but pointed to Ms. Sweet. "This is Courtney Sweet and her son Jesse." She reversed her gaze and finger and said, "This is Richard Shipton and his daughter Avery."

Courtney smiled. "Richard? Hmmm, how fitting. I bet you go by Di—"

"Richard," he snapped. "I go by Richard." He looked at his watch. "Can we get on with this? I've got to find a dentist for my daughter."

The principal explained that while she didn't usually suspend kids their age, the nature of the fight and the injuries resulting were severe enough that she was considering it.

"Perfect. First the teeth and now a suspension? Now, what am I going to do?" He pulled his phone out of his pocket and started searching for a dentist.

"I'm not suspending them this time," Principal Cain said. "But any more trouble and they'll get a full week."

"Avery, you need to apologize."

"I'm sorry, Daddy, but he's not a nice boy."

"I meant, apologize to Principal Cain."

Avery said a nearly silent "I'm sorry."

Richard looked at Courtney. "There's this saying about apples and trees." He ended it there when Courtney gave him a scathing look. Her expression softened when she looked at his daughter.

"If you're looking for a dentist, go to Smith. He's good with kids." She opened her purse and pulled out her wallet. In seconds, she handed him a business card.

He stared at her. "Why would I trust your opinion?"

"Because I have a dentist, and you don't." She turned to Jesse. "Smile, honey." Jesse smiled. "My son has teeth. Nice ones at that."

He swiped the card from her hand. "This works out perfectly, because they'll know where to send the bill."

"What?"

He took Avery's hand and walked toward the door. "This is your fault. You should have raised your son not to hit girls."

She stomped after him to the parking lot. "Don't forget, she threw the first rock."

He opened the door to the SUV. "And he threw the last one." He turned to his daughter. "Get in the car, Avery."

"Hey," Courtney said. "Don't take this out on her. It's not her fault."

He raised a brow. "At least we agree on something." After Avery buckled herself in, he shut the door, rounded the Suburban, and took a seat behind the wheel before gunning the engine and driving away.

THANKFULLY, this was an emergency, and Dr. Smith was able to see them right away.

As soon as they arrived, they were ushered into an office, where x-rays were taken, and an exam was done.

Richard felt like a horrible father because he couldn't answer many of the dentist's questions. He didn't know when Avery's last cleaning happened and had no idea who her former dentist was, or if she was up to date with her immunizations. Since Cadence's death, he barely managed to keep it all together. Being a pilot kept him on the go constantly, and finding dependable childcare options was difficult.

His life's motto was taken straight out of Avery's favorite movie ... just keep swimming.

"What are we looking at?" Richard asked.

"This is a long-term issue. She's too young for a permanent fix because her jaw will grow through adolescence. Once she stops growing, we can look at implants. For now, I'd suggest something like a flipper."

Avery spoke. "Fwipper? What's that?" With her two front teeth missing, she couldn't make an L sound.

The dentist explained the retainer-like device, which was the only alternative for her to have teeth.

That was it then. They'd wait for the swelling to go down, and then she'd be fitted for a retainer with two fake teeth.

"Who can we thank for referring you?" Dr. Smith asked as he led them to the front desk.

Richard grunted. "Thank? Oh, I wouldn't thank Courtney Sweet." He stared at his daughter's swollen lips. At least the teeth were taken out at the root, and her pretty little face wasn't cut in the process. "Just keep swimming, right?"

"Courtney? She's a lovely woman, and Jesse is such a good boy."

"I can't say." He tried to think of all the negative things about her, but there wasn't much in truth. She'd tried to be friendly, and he wasn't Mr. Sunshine. On any other day, her sassiness would have been entertaining, but currently, it annoyed him. Maybe because, while he tried to dislike her on so many levels, her biggest drawback was that she had a son with good aim.

The dentist left him at the desk with a woman named Maggie who made their next appointment and told him the fee due that day.

"The bill goes to Mrs. Sweet." While the principal called her miss, he couldn't imagine she wasn't married. She had that stay-at-home-mom vibe to her with the paint-splattered sweats and sensible haircut. She wasn't like the other women on the trail that morning who looked more plastic than Barbie. Courtney was real.

"Oh, I'm sorry, I can't charge another client for services you received."

He pulled out his credit card and laid it on the counter. "That's fine. Can I have a printout of the bill and estimates for future care? I'll give it to her myself." He figured he could have Avery's babysitter drop it off at the school, and the school could deliver it. Part of him felt they had some culpability, so they could be the go-between.

Maggie printed out the bill and the estimate, which he tucked into his side pocket.

He held Avery's hand and walked her to the car. "Are you hungry, little bird?"

She nodded.

"I imagine you'll want something soft for a few days." He sat in the driver's seat. "How about the diner downtown. They have soup and ice cream."

Avery was all in for the ice cream.

He parked in front of A Dollop of Delight bakery, which sat

two doors down from the diner. As he rounded the Suburban to get Avery, a familiar face stared out of the window—Courtney. He didn't seem to be able to escape the woman.

He pulled the estimate from his pocket, took Avery's hand, and walked her inside. Courtney stood staring at him.

"Are you kidding me?" she asked. "What are the odds?"

CHAPTER THREE

Courtney stared at Richard, waiting for him to say something.

"There are too many variables to calculate, but I'd say they're pretty good since we're here." He repeated exactly what she'd told him hours ago.

"You're like gum on the bottom of a shoe. I can't seem to scrape you off."

"Maybe, but I'm good gum and nice shoes." He slipped his hand inside his pocket and pulled something from it. "Avery is limited on what she can eat, and so we decided soup and ice cream from the diner would be good."

She glanced at the little girl whose pigtails were wonky with one high and one low. She had on a plaid skirt with a polka dot shirt and striped socks. The kid was a mess. Either her mother was missing from the picture, or she was an independent dresser.

Courtney lowered herself in front of Avery. "Are you okay?"

Avery nodded and smiled. Her lip was still red and swollen, and the place where her two front teeth used to be was raw and angry looking.

Courtney hadn't taken the time to take in the implications of what had happened. Her agitation at the father had made her overlook that a child was involved.

"I'm so sorry this happened to you." She held her hand out and the little girl took it. "How about a cookie?" She looked up at Richard. "I realize she probably can't bite it, but maybe you can take it to the diner and get her some milk to soften it."

"I'm not sure a cookie falls in with the dietary guidelines for healthy eating," he said.

"And ice cream does?"

"Hey," he said. "It's dairy."

Courtney led Avery to the counter. "Cookies have dairy too. Real butter. Comes from cows. You should look it up."

Avery laughed. "She's funny."

Or that was what Courtney thought she said. Fs would be difficult without front teeth.

"Oh, yeah," Richard said with sarcasm. "She's a laugh a minute."

"Can she have a cookie or not?"

Avery turned on her girlish charm and looked at her father with pleading eyes.

"I suppose it's fine. We're breaking all the rules today."

"Well, then, let's go all in, and you can pick one for your father too. He could use a little sweet to tone down his bitterness."

"I'm not bitter."

"Says you." She walked Avery behind the counter. "Which one do you want?"

There were dozens of cookies in the case. Where there used to be loaves of bread, there were now cookies and cakes and cupcakes and pies. The bread was still available but showcased in baskets on the wall.

Entering her brother into the baking contest changed everything for him and the family. Chloe Mason may have won the contest, but her brother won Chloe's heart, and the bakery was transformed.

"When I said we're breaking all the rules, I didn't mean I was up for theft. Should you be behind the counter?"

Feeling smug, she smiled and said, "I own the bakery."

It wasn't an out-and-out lie. She was part owner—the smallest part. With Chloe investing her winnings, she and her brother Gage owned the lion's share of the bakery. Her mother held a part-time job and Courtney had a small stake in the bakery, which was just in the black, according to the books. They basically made enough money to pay everyone a small salary and keep the lights on.

Avery pointed to the princess cookie with the blue icing and sparkles.

"That's an excellent choice. I would have picked the same." Courtney looked up at Richard, who looked like he'd sucked on a lemon.

"How about this one for your father. Seems fitting." It was a bran cookie. "Maybe it will help him digest the situation better."

She took a waxed paper from the box and picked up the cookie and handed it to Richard.

"Can we trade?" He thrust his hand forward and gave her the estimate.

"What's this?"

"It's the bill for today and an estimate of things to come."

"You came here to give me a bill?"

He shook his head. "No, as I said before, I was taking Avery to the diner. It was a fortuitous accident that we parked out front of the bakery, and I saw you in the window."

She led Avery out from behind the counter before unfolding the paper.

She looked at the numbers, and her jaw nearly hit the floor.

"Retainers with teeth? Future implants?"

"It's what it costs." He shrugged.

She stomped her foot. "With these costs, I should be able to knock a few of your teeth out too." Her voice rose an octave from the beginning of the sentence to the end, and Jesse raced out from the back room.

He slid to a stop in front of Avery, and she watched with amusement at the way her son's cheeks blushed. Avery might hate him, but he liked her.

"Oh, it's you," he said with no hint of unhappiness to see her.

"Go away." She covered her mouth with her hand. "I look ugly."

"You ... you ..." He couldn't seem to come up with the words.

"Beauty comes from the inside," Courtney said. "The most gorgeous of beasts," she lifted her eyes to look at Richard, "can be hideous if they are ugly inside. I can see that you are pretty inside and out." She bopped her nose with the tip of her finger. "I hope you stay that way."

That last part was meant for her father because children often mimicked their parents' behavior, and she didn't want the sweet part of Avery, if there was any, to be marred by her father's bad behavior.

She stared at the numbers again, and her heartbeat shifted from already racing to pedal to the metal speeding. There was no way she could afford this.

"Let's go, Avery." He held out his hand, and she tucked hers into his. "I bet you're starving."

"I'm starving too, Mom," Jesse said. "Can we go to the diner too?"

She glanced at the paper in her hands.

18

"Sorry, kiddo, it doesn't look like we're going anywhere for a long time."

He let his shoulders slump forward. "Awww. We never get to do anything fun."

"I wouldn't have pegged you for the fun-sucker kind of woman."

"Says the man who dims the sun the minute he goes outside." She scrunched her nose.

He laughed and walked a few steps back before handing the cookie back to her. "You may need this more than me. You've got that constipated look to your face that my wife used to have when she was unhappy."

"I bet that was often. Where is she now? Avoiding your sunshine and rainbows personality?"

His blue eyes turned cloudy and dark, and his lips fell into a frown.

"I'm a widower." He walked back to Avery and swept her into his arms before walking out the door.

All that sparring with Richard was invigorating until that moment. As she watched the two of them walk down the sidewalk toward the diner, she felt as small as the tiniest ant.

Of all the things she tried to teach Jesse, the most important was to be a good human, and she'd shown her worst side.

She folded the paper in half and put it in her pocket. She'd figure out a way to pay for Avery's dental bills.

"You like her, don't you?"

Jesse looked appalled. "What? No way. She's a girl."

"Yes, I noticed."

"Girls are gross."

She laughed. "I'm a girl."

He shook his head. "Nope, you're a mom."

There was some truth to that. Once she became a mom, most

of the girl things went away. As a single mom, she didn't have the time or resources for girls' nights out and spa days. Not that she ever had those. She did have her nails done once, and it felt like she'd been crowned queen for a day.

"We need to talk about what happened."

Jesse groaned. "I already wrote I'm sorry five hundred times."

It was a punishment passed down for generations. As a child, she'd written an inappropriate word on her hand, and her mother made her write it five hundred times. She'd done the same with Jesse. The repetitive exercise would help him remember not to make those mistakes again—or so she hoped.

"You know what, Jesse? I don't need your sorry, but Avery does. Those were her permanent teeth, so they won't grow back." She patted her pocket. "Now I have to pay for that mistake, which means things are going to be a little lean for the next ... oh, let's say ... I should have it paid off by the time you go to college."

Jesse was a good boy, and he understood more than an average kid his age.

"But she threw the rock first."

How did she teach a boy to become a man when she'd never been one? How did she show him how to defend himself but understand that sometimes it was best to walk away?

"I told you never to hit a girl."

He frowned. "I didn't hit her. The rock did."

It was going to be a long night.

The bell above the door chimed, and her brother and Chloe walked inside.

"Thanks for watching the store while we grabbed a bite to eat," Chloe said.

"Yeah, sis. Thanks. Did anything exciting happen while we were gone?" Gage asked.

"Oh, you know, just the normal. I sparred with a customer, got a bill I can't afford, and failed at parenting. It's just another good day in the life of Mama Sweet." She pointed to the back room. "Get your stuff, Jesse. We've got to get going."

"You okay?" her brother asked as soon as Jesse was gone.

She breathed deeply and exhaled.

"I'm a Sweet. We're made with kindness and sprinkled with sugar. I'm good."

Jesse ran from the back room, tugging his backpack over his shoulder.

"Mom, I'm hungry. Can we eat at the diner?"

She had a twenty in her pocket and a few hundred in her bank account. Though her bookkeeping sense told her it wasn't wise, her downtrodden inner self couldn't argue with a night of no cooking or dishes.

"Yep, but we're headed to debtors' prison, so treat it like your last meal and choose wisely."

She waved her hand over her head to say goodbye and walked to the door.

"What's that all about?" she heard Chloe ask.

"Who knows," Gage said. "She's always been a little dramatic. She was the president of the drama club."

Courtney wished she could blame her dramatic answer on her inner thespian, but the bill in her pocket for several hundred dollars now and four figures down the road was the cause of her theatrics. How was she going to come up with that?

"I'll sell a kidney," she said as she left the bakery.

Hand in hand, she and Jesse walked two doors down to the diner. It wasn't your usual fifties-themed place but a real hole-in-the-wall dive that offered eggs and toast all day long for ninety-nine cents. They got you on the bacon and coffee, which were two dollars and ninety-nine cents each.

"Avery and her father are going to be there, and I want you on your best behavior. No throwing anything."

Jesse huffed. "I won't. I'm not that stupid."

She opened the door to the diner and was hit with multiple smells, but the strongest was grilled onions. It always amazed her how something that could make you shed a thousand tears when raw could smell so darned good grilled.

Chloe had recently taught her to cut the onions on a wet paper towel, and that soaked up whatever it was that caused the tears. She was initially skeptical but believed that a person should try all legal things once, and it worked. Her onion cutting was forever changed.

The two of them stood at the front of the diner, looking for an empty seat. Sadly, there were no open tables. The only place to go was the counter, which was occupied by Richard and Avery.

She stood tall and pulled her shoulders back before taking Jesse to the only two seats available. She took the one next to Richard while Jesse sat to her right. It seemed prudent to keep the kids separated. Then again, she had to admit that Richard brought out the worst in her. He was an attractive man who, when nearby, made her consider a lifetime behind bars for murder.

He turned to glance her way. "Stalking is still against the law."

She tucked her hands under her thighs and smiled in his direction. "Eating is still legal, and my son is hungry. No law against taking the last two seats in the restaurant."

He returned her smile, but just like hers, she imagined it wasn't genuine. She'd seen his eyes get angry and grow stormy, so by deduction, she figured they would sparkle like aquamarines lit by the sun when he smiled sincerely.

"You own a bakery." He lifted a brow. "Is the food not good?"

She gasped. "Of course, it's good. I'm a Sweet, and I don't do anything halfway."

"That's a trait that must run in the family."

"If Avery were in Little League, maybe the tables would have been turned."

"We don't have time for sports. I barely have time to get her dressed and ready for school."

She leaned around him to peek at his daughter. "You're dressing her?" She laughed. "Figures."

"It's a joint effort."

She took in the mix and match attire. "You know, you are the parent in this relationship."

He sighed. "What's wrong with what she's wearing?"

"Are you colorblind?"

CHAPTER FOUR

He raised his hand and asked for the check. This was a complete replay of his marriage. Everything went to shit because of one personal deficit.

He turned to face Courtney. "As a matter of fact, I am colorblind, which is why I can only fly regional aircraft and only during the day. It's also why I'm not on exciting long-haul trips that provide more perks like fabulous jump seats to Europe to shop in Paris. It's why my significant other found another, and then ..." He shook his head.

Disgust filled him. He wasn't sure where all the vitriol came from, but he'd been bottling his agitation for years, and it was finally getting ready to spill over the edge.

Was it his shame at not providing what Cadence needed that weighed him down, or was it knowing that his colorblindness seemed to ruin everything in his life? Maybe his most recent agitation came because he somehow thought he owed this woman an explanation when he owed her nothing.

"You don't need the story of my life."

Her expression was as empty as the runway after the last plane of the night touched down.

"I'm sorry." A crease between her brows formed. "I don't know what to say."

He took cash from his wallet to pay his bill and set both on the counter. "I bet that's a rarity for you."

"Look, you don't have to be rude."

He spun his seat around to face Avery, giving Courtney his back. "You ready, sweetie?" He didn't have to be rude, but he also didn't have to go out of his way to be nice. Courtney Sweet was like a piece of lint he couldn't get off his pants. No matter how much he tried, she was there, hanging around and annoying him.

As he and Avery stood to leave, he turned to Courtney. "Enjoy your meal."

He was almost at the door when Courtney called his name. "Richard." He wasn't up for more sparring or idle chitchat, so he raised his hand in a dismissive wave.

He had to work tomorrow, and his uniforms weren't pressed. Avery needed a bath, and obviously, they needed a new plan for mixing and matching her clothes. Painful as it was to admit, his daughter was a modern-day Pippi Longstocking with her fashion sense, bad hair, and lack of color coordination.

They walked hand in hand to his car and, once inside, headed toward home.

"Do you have homework?"

Her groan was his answer.

"You'd think I'd get a homework pass because I lost two teeth."

"Life doesn't work that way. There will always be expectations. Those you put on yourself, which are often the hardest to achieve. Those from society, which are mostly common-sense things like don't lie, steal, or cheat." When he said the word cheat, it had a very different meaning than what he knew his daughter would think about. "And those expectations put on you by others. For example, I expect you to always do your best in school. I also expect you not to throw rocks at boys you like."

He took his eyes off the road for a second. It was long enough to notice the blush rising to her cheeks.

"I don't like him. Jesse Sweet is a stupid boy with stupid curls in his hair and a space between his teeth. He always wears ugly anime T-shirts, and his tennis shoes have a tear near the white rubber toe thingy."

He tried to hold back a laugh.

"Oh, yeah, I can see that you don't pay him much mind. He's ugly and smells bad, too."

"No, Daddy." She shook her head. "He always smells like cinnamon." As soon as she realized what she said, she added. "But he is ugly."

"Of course. About as ugly as his mother." Who wasn't ugly at all. Courtney Sweet was a Bratz doll with her blonde hair, curvy figure, and big blue eyes, but she didn't have that high-maintenance look about her. Nope, she was single-mom Bratz or down-on-her-luck Bratz or girl-next-door Bratz. She was equally intriguing and irritating and definitely off-limits because his life was complicated enough.

As he pulled into the driveway of the house, something didn't feel right. It was that feeling he got during flight checks when something was missing.

"Damn it." His hand flew to his pocket to find it empty. "My wallet."

Avery groaned. "Does that mean we have to go back?"

He hated to keep her out later than necessary, but he couldn't fly without his ID, and he had the flight from Vail to Denver and back twice tomorrow.

"I'm sorry, sweetheart, but I've got to have my identification card."

She crossed her arms with a harrumph and slid down into the seat. He was sure she'd collect in a pile of goo on the floor.

"Fine. But can I have more ice cream?" She turned and smiled at him. Her sore gums reminded him that she'd had a rough day.

"Are you in pain?"

She rubbed her gumline with her tongue. "Nope, that shot the dentist gave me is still working."

He needed to remember to give her the pain meds in an hour, so they weren't trying to catch up with pain relief.

"I'll tell you what, how about I give you a popsicle? The cold will be good, and since it's fruit juice, I'll feel like I'm a halfway decent dad."

"You're a good daddy, and I love you."

He reached over and tugged one of her pigtails. "I love you too, little bird." When Avery was younger, she was convinced her name was Aviary, and that's when he started calling her little bird. He actually called her pigeon, but she succinctly informed him that pigeons were not pretty, and because she was, she couldn't be one of those.

They drove back to the diner. He wanted to lock the doors and tell Avery to stay put, but there were so many horror stories about kids being left in cars and the perils they faced, so they went into the diner together and found the counter empty.

He was one hundred percent certain that when Courtney called his name, she was letting him know he'd forgotten his wallet. Now he felt shitty that he waved her off when she was only trying to help.

"Can I help you?" the older waitress asked.

Richard pointed to himself. "Do you remember me?" He

pointed to the third stool from the end of the counter. "I sat there with my daughter tonight but I left my wallet. Do you have it?"

The silver-haired waitress tapped her chin and smiled.

"Nope. I don't, but Courtney probably does. In fact, I think she called you, but you didn't hear her."

Oh, he heard her but ignored her. He'd learned that little trick from his wife.

He could hear Cadence loud and clear yelling at him. "Didn't you hear me?" He always heard her, but in truth, he didn't listen well. After years of fighting, her voice became background noise.

He looked back to the counter as if somehow Courtney and Jesse would magically appear, but their stools remained empty.

"You might be able to catch someone at the bakery before it closes."

"Right. The bakery." He glanced at his watch and saw it was nearing six. The day had gotten away from him. "Let's see if we can catch them, kiddo." He practically tugged Avery into a sprint to the bakery two doors down.

A man pulled the door shut and locked it when he arrived.

"Hey," Richard shouted.

The guy spun around and lifted his hands into a boxer's stance. Only one hand was empty, and the other held keys and what looked like a bag of bread.

"I don't have money, man. You're hitting the wrong location."

Richard stared at him, trying to process the situation. "Hitting?" It dawned on him that the man thought he was robbing him. Richard moved Avery in front of him. "Do you think I'd rob you with my daughter in tow?"

"You should never lie, steal, or cheat," Avery piped in. "We're here because my dad needs his card."

The guy relaxed his stance. "All good rules to live by." He

looked between them. "I'm not following you about the card, though."

Richard wiped his hand on his pants because, with a ten-year-old girl, he never knew what was on hers. Once he'd looked down to find a magic marker that had seemingly melted from her hand to his. Chocolate did the same. And then there was the glitter. There was always glitter. Every cockpit he flew in had glitter embedded into the carpet.

"I'm Richard Shipton, and this is my daughter, Avery."

The man's mouth twisted and morphed into a smile. He pointed to Richard. "Obnoxious jogger?" Then he glanced down at Avery. "First love?" After shaking his head, he chuckled. "Sorry, it had to hurt so much, kiddo." His eyes lifted. "You must be looking for Courtney."

Finally, they were getting somewhere. "Yes, the owner of the bakery."

The man offered his hand. "I'm Gage, and it's a family-run bakery, so while Courtney doesn't own it outright, she has a stake in it. She's our bookkeeper."

Why had she portrayed herself differently, or had she? Was it just another example of hearing what he wanted to hear, or was that what she wanted him to think?

"She has my wallet. Did she happen to leave it in the bakery?"

Gage looked at the door as if he could see the wallet clearly and shook his head. "Haven't seen a wallet lying around. Did you leave it in the bakery?"

"No, I left it in the diner."

Gage furrowed his brow. "I'm typically not dimwitted, but if you left your wallet in the diner, why would it be here?"

He could see how confusing it was becoming, and he opened his mouth to speak, but Avery stomped her foot and spoke first.

"Are you paying attention? We were at the diner. Ms.

Courtney and stupid Jesse were at the diner. Daddy left his wallet there. Courtney has it."

Gage looked at Richard in shock. "It starts that early?"

Richard knew he was talking about the attitude. "You have no idea, man. I swear they are born with that stomping foot, hands on the hips, and snark oozing from everywhere thing."

There was a moment of silence. "Well, you can see that Court isn't here. So, I can't help you. She usually stops in after she drops Jesse at school. You can check back then."

Richard's heart took on one powerful beat and skipped the next. "That won't work. I'm on shift tomorrow morning. I need my wallet. Without it, I can't get through airport security. Can you tell me where she lives? I'll swing by and grab it."

"I'm not telling you where my sister lives." He stared at Richard for a moment and then at Avery, who gave him the puppy-dog eyes that always made Richard melt. "Tell you what. Let me call her. If she says it's okay, then I'll point you in the right direction."

Gage took his phone from his pocket and dialed a number.

"Hey, Court, I've got a guy here who says you have his wallet."

There were muffled words he couldn't hear clearly.

"I told him, but apparently, he's got to fly in the morning and needs his wallet."

More words seemed to string together, but none he could make out except maybe jerk.

"I'm not telling him that. He wants to swing by your place to pick it up. Can I give him your address?" He put his hand over the phone. "She's not all that happy."

"At least she's consistent," Richard said.

Gage held the phone from his ear.

"I'm not telling him that, either. You realize his daughter is here. You two can figure all that out. Address? Yes or no?" He tapped his foot, waiting for his sister to answer. "Okay." He hung up. "She said that I could give it to you, but only because your daughter is cute, and she's saving her from spending extra time with you if you should have to call in sick because you lost your wallet."

"How generous."

"She lives at 333 Witches Coven Way, Unit 3."

"Thanks, man. I owe you one."

Gage laughed. "We'll square up some other time. I'll see if you survive tonight." He turned and walked down the street. A few stores away, a homeless man sat begging. Gage kneeled in front of him and handed over the bag he'd been carrying. The Sweets were a confusing lot.

He and Avery rushed to the address Gage passed on. He half expected to see her out front, winding up a pitch to lob it at him as he passed, but she wasn't there, so they got out of the car and walked up the sidewalk to her unit. This area of Timberline was older, and the place where she lived probably was some sort of rental cabin in its day. The stacked log exterior was quaint. The carved bear at the entrance holding a welcome sign made it homey.

He lifted his hand to knock, and the door opened.

"Good evening, Mr. Shipton, come inside. My mom should be done screaming into her pillow in a moment. I'll tell her you're here."

He'd laugh if it wasn't so surprising. Not only the openness of Jesse, but the fact that Courtney was at a stage of frustration that required a pillow scream.

Then there was the fact that he was now standing in Courtney Sweet's house. It smelled like cinnamon and sugar, and he could see why Avery picked up on the scent right away. It was like coming home to grandma's house on a snowy day and getting a warm, freshly baked cookie. Not that Courtney was in the grandma category. If she were, she'd be a hot one.

"I told you not to let strangers into the house." Courtney reprimanded Jesse and walked into the living room.

"He's not a stranger, Mom. We've spent most of the day together." Jesse shoved his hands in his pockets and looked at the floor. "Can I offer Avery a cookie?"

Courtney sighed. "Yes. Always be a good host."

Avery slipped from his side and happily followed her nemesis into the kitchen.

"Is that okay with you?"

He looked past her.

"Kind of late now since Jesse already poured the milk."

She smiled. It was the first genuine smile he'd seen from her, and it nearly knocked him on his backside. She was beautiful, but then again, bees were beautiful but had a painful sting.

"I'm sorry about that. I'm usually more considerate when it comes to parenting and asking first."

He shrugged. "I hear it takes a village to raise a kid."

She lifted her hands into the air, revival style. "Amen to that. I don't know what I'd do without my mother and Gage. Now we have Chloe, so there's more support."

Envy bit at his raw edges. "There's just me. I mean, I've got a few sitters that I hire, but good people are hard to find."

"That's what I've heard. I'm lucky to work mostly from home. It keeps it cheap and easy." She looked around her place as if seeing it for the first time like he was.

She didn't have the uncomfortable formal sofa that made your back ache the second a person sat in it. Nope, Courtney's place was decorated with overstuffed leather chairs and a couch. Plaid pillows brought in patches of color to the worn brown of the furniture. Everything looked toward a big stone fireplace where pictures of her and Jesse dotted the mantel. There was a closed pine cabinet that sat at an angle in the corner. Richard would bet his next paycheck that her TV was tucked nicely inside. He'd also bet that it was rarely used. Courtney seemed like the board game or let's read kind of mom. Cadence was the mani-pedi and let's watch the *Real Housewives of Beverly Hills* kind of mom.

"Forgive my manners. Would you like a cookie?" Courtney asked.

He glanced at Avery, who enthusiastically nodded her head. "The boss says yes, so I'd love one."

It was an awkward moment. If he wasn't fighting with Courtney, he didn't know how to act. He'd never been uncomfortable with women, but she knocked him off-kilter.

"Milk or coffee?" She walked into the kitchen and placed a cookie on a napkin and set it on the edge of the island in front of a stool. "Have a seat."

He took the stool but declined the drink. "We have to get going. Avery has homework, and I have domestic things to take care of."

She lifted her eyes. "So, the wife managed to domesticate you. Was that hard?"

He could have been offended, but he wasn't. "Oh, I'm still in training." He nodded toward Avery. "Each owner brings its own set of challenges."

"I imagine that's true."

He wanted to know more about her but didn't want to ask the pointed questions in front of her son.

"Jesse's father?" He hoped that was basic enough but not too intrusive. There was no sign of a man in the house. Not a picture was up that included anyone beyond Gage and Jesse, and an older couple he assumed were her parents.

"Not in the picture." Her eyes followed his line of sight to the mantel. "Literally. He was gone before it all began."

"No one since?"

"Who needs someone when I've got him?" She looked at her son with such love and affection that he was almost jealous of the kid. His eyes skimmed across the stone counter to where his wallet lay on a book.

"Right. The wallet." She picked it up and handed it to him, exposing the title of a tattered book called *Recipes for Love*. "Is this the new plan? Since the morning exercise group was a wash, you'll bake up something perfect?"

"I didn't go to the group looking for love. I was hoping to find a friend."

He smiled, so she knew he was teasing. "Next time, leave your broom at home."

Her jaw dropped. "You did not just call me a witch."

"You live on a street called Witches Coven and have a book of love spells." He reached for the book, but she snatched it away before he could open it.

"It's a recipe book. I think. Best be careful, or I might bring out my crystal ball and bubbling cauldron. Who knows what I can summon?"

He laughed. "I've seen you angry, and I'd believe you have the power to make it rain fire."

She smiled again, and his heart thumped so hard he was afraid he'd bruised a chamber or two.

"Oh, you haven't seen me angry yet."

He pointed to the book. "I'd stick with that then. Love is always better than the alternative."

"I bet you know a lot about love."

He glanced at his daughter, who was in a deep discussion with Jesse about the best Disney movie.

"Oh, I know enough to stay away from anything resembling it."

She cocked her head and frowned. "Looks like we went to the same school."

He stared at the book she held to her chest. "And yet you cling to the idea of it."

After a long sigh, she put the book down.

"I honestly can't tell you where this book came from. It appeared in my backpack one day out of nowhere, almost like magic. In fact, I haven't even opened it. As far as love goes. I'm not looking for it either. It may be for some, but when they were giving out hearts, I think I was holding the door for everyone, and when it was my turn to get one, mine was trampled by the masses and already torn."

The kids got into a screaming match about movies, with Avery telling Jesse that *Finding Nemo* was the finest movie ever made. He fought back and told her it was something called *The Apple Dumpling Gang.*

"Looks like we should go, or there may be another dentist appointment in one of our futures." He folded the napkin around his cookie. "I'll eat this later." He stood and looked at his daughter with a loving but stern look. "Avery, let's go."

She huffed. "Boys are so stupid."

He nodded. "Yes, we are." He was feeling stupid in all ways just then. He'd done so many things wrong that day. "I'm sorry for not listening when you called me."

She laughed. "So, you heard me, and chose to ignore me."

He nodded. "Boys can be so stupid."

"Is it possible we agree on something?"

CHAPTER FIVE

As Courtney packed the cookies into an airtight container, she stared at *Recipes for Love*. She had no idea how she got it, though she figured it was probably Chloe who'd snuck it in her bag.

Courtney didn't have much of a life and spent most of her time at home, Jesse's school, or the bakery. There was a slim chance her friend Rebecca had slipped it into her bag when they met for coffee a few weeks ago, but she was reasonably sure she would've noticed it.

"Did you enjoy Avery's visit?" she asked Jesse, who sat at the island doing his math homework.

He frowned. "No, I did not. She's a pain in my..."

Courtney lifted a brow, waiting for Jesse to finish the sentence. "In your what?"

He pressed his palms to his temples. "She makes my head hurt. Besides, she spit milk when she laughed."

Courtney smiled. "Bet she didn't do that when she had teeth."

He hung his head. "I feel bad. I didn't know I'd knock out her teeth."

She moved around the counter and hugged him.

"That's the thing about emotions. Sometimes they get the better of you. Those Shiptons are frustrating." She didn't want him to think it was okay, so she added, "We have to think before we react. Nothing good ever came out of anger."

"But that's it. I wasn't angry when I threw the rock. I was just..." He frowned.

"You reacted without thinking about the consequences. I did a bit of that myself today, with my words. I didn't know Avery's mother died, and I felt bad when I said something rude to Mr. Shipton in the diner."

"That happened in third grade. Avery used to cry a lot."

She didn't realize how long they'd known each other. "You like Avery, don't you?"

His earlobes turned crimson. Embarrassment always heated his face, and those red lobes were a dead giveaway.

"Yuck, Mom. She's a girl. And she has no front teeth."

Courtney shook her head. "Which is your fault." Rather than pressing her point about him liking a girl, she moved in another direction—a teaching opportunity. "You may think girls are yucky right now, but one day, some girl is going to steal your heart, and when that happens, you won't think girls are all that bad."

He smiled. "Avery isn't all that bad."

That was as close to a confession as she was going to get.

She put the cookies in the cupboard and made a cup of tea before sitting next to Jesse.

While he worked diligently on his homework, she opened the tattered cookbook and read the hand-written note on the inside front cover. The book was more like a journal of sorts. The kind of cookbook passed down from generation to generation.

Dear Baker,

Everything I learned about love, I learned from baking.

Everything you need to know about love, you'll learn here.

Because if you're reading this, it means you've accepted the challenge of choosing one recipe, perfecting it, and passing on the book.

As with everything in life, baking takes effort. Like love, it can't be rushed.

Have you ever wondered why baked goods require certain ingredients?

We add sugar to bring out our inner sweetness.

Salt gives life its flavor.

Flour is a binder like honesty and faithfulness.

Butter is the guilty pleasure in the mix.

Baking soda lifts like a bright smile on a dull day.

Without these, a cake is not a cake, and a pie is not a pie. Without love, life isn't worth living.

Baking, like love, should be done with passion.

I challenge you to pick one recipe and only one because love shouldn't be hoarded but shared.

Choose the right recipe, and if you can't decide, open the book to a page and let the recipe choose you.

Share the dessert but not the book. There will be time for that later.

Remember, a perfect cake, or pie, or cookie is like perfect love. It takes practice, patience, give and take, resourcefulness, perseverance, and often teamwork.

With love,

Adelaide Phelps

Courtney laughed. It wasn't her ability to love that was the issue. Her problem was she couldn't get a man to stay around long enough to see that she was worthy of love, which in the end made her question if that was true.

She knew how to love. She loved Jesse with all her might. Every ounce of her being loved that boy.

She skimmed through the recipes with names like Slow Burn Blondie, Romantic Flame Flan, and Treasure Me Truffles. Wouldn't it be great if all she had to do was whip up a batch of Cherish Me Cheesecake to find a perfect man?

"Doesn't exist."

"What doesn't exist?" Jesse asked.

"Perfection," she said, thinking quickly. "None of us are perfect, but it's important to always be your best."

Once Jesse finished his homework and showered, they had a little snuggle time on the sofa while he read her a new sci-fi book he'd borrowed from the library.

After the day she'd had, she was exhausted and fell into bed too.

———

"I DON'T BELIEVE YOU." Courtney pushed the chair from the desk and stretched her back. She always got a kink in her neck when she bent over the bakery's books for hours.

"You can believe what you want," Chloe said, "But I don't remember a cookbook." Her future sister-in-law's smile was hard to read, but there was a glint of mischief to it.

"Fine, but don't be a meddler. No one likes those. Besides, the love train passed my station long ago. No one's looking for a single broke mother of one with stretch marks and a disagreeable temperament."

Chloe leaned against the doorjamb. "Don't count yourself out. There's something for everyone. Some men like big booties, some like cute feet. I bet there's a man out there who would love to rile you up and get a glimpse of your temper."

"My temper is on empty right now. I spent all my anger yesterday on Richard Shipton."

Chloe smiled. "You know … when I met your brother, I wasn't a fan."

Courtney waved her off. "Yeah, I know. You guys had that love/hate thing going."

"Nope, it was a hate/hate thing going, and then somehow we figured out we weren't much different. Sometimes, when you look at a person, and they are a mirror of yourself, it's hard to accept what you're seeing."

"How did you figure that out?" Courtney closed the ledger and tucked it back into the drawer. Sales were better since they rebranded and offered more selection, but they were far from becoming the next million-dollar sensation.

"Your brother was driven to win, and so was I. Once we realized that fighting each other got us nowhere, we started working together. The world is hard enough on its own. We were both trying to prove something. We taught each other that we didn't need the validation of others to know we were good enough."

"I'm glad you didn't kill each other in the process."

"What about this Richard guy? There are some sparks there, right?"

Courtney stared at Chloe like she was speaking a foreign language. "Sparks? Until last night, if he were fuel, I would have struck a match and watched him burn. The man is frustrating as hell. He's…"

"He's what?"

"He's…"

Chloe smiled. "Yes?"

"He's a mess. I thought my life was bad, but he's a colorblind pilot and a widower with a ten-year-old girl who dresses like she's homeless." She shrugged. "Who cares if he's handsome and has eyes like a cloudless sky? It's not like I was checking him out, but he isn't bad in sweatpants, and that five-o'clock shadow is pure sin. Poor kid probably gets pizza for dinner daily." She shook her head. "Probably not pizza because he doesn't have an ounce of fat on him." When she looked up to find Chloe smiling, she knew she'd said too much. "What?"

"Maybe there's something you can teach each other. Stop fighting with the man and figure out how to work together."

"Sure." She resisted the urge to roll her eyes. "Promise to bail me out of jail when I attempt to murder him."

"Now that's what I call passion." Chloe walked away.

Courtney glanced at the clock and swore under her breath. She was late picking up Jesse. Where had the time gone? She grabbed her bag and keys and swiped a couple of cookies before she ran out the door.

If Jesse got upset at her tardiness, at least she'd have a peace offering.

When she got to the school, she found Jesse and Avery sitting together on the bench outside. Principal Cain hovered over them.

"I can't get a hold of your father, Avery."

"He's flying today. Ms. Britney was supposed to pick me up." Her little lip quivered.

"Hey, buddy," Courtney said as she ran forward. "I'm sorry I'm late."

Mrs. Cain looked at her watch and frowned. "One down and one to go." Her expression was dour, like she'd sucked lemons. "If your father doesn't get here in five minutes, I'll have to call someone."

Courtney got the feeling that the "someone" Principal Cain was referring to was the authorities. She could see the tears pool in the corners of Avery's eyes, and her heart ached for the girl. Right then, she knew she had to do something.

"Avery, don't you remember? You're supposed to go home with us," she lied. "That was the deal your father and I made last night when you guys came over."

"I am?"

Courtney smiled, hoping the principal wouldn't see through her fib. She glanced down at the cookies in her hand. Fortuitously, she had grabbed two.

"I brought you both a cookie. Grab your things and let's go. It's spaghetti night."

Jesse let out a whoop. "I love spaghetti night. Can we have meat sauce?"

"You bet." She tried to get the kids to move it along before the principal questioned the validity of her untruth.

"You aren't listed on Avery's file as someone who can pick her up."

This time she rolled her eyes most exaggeratedly. "You think I'm trying to kidnap her? What parent in their right mind would voluntarily put these two together? I'm not a glutton for punishment, but there is a big dental bill, and this is how I'm paying it off." She shrugged. "But if you'd rather wait until Richard gets back from his flight, we can. I think he said he'd be home around dinner time." She turned to Avery and winked. "Isn't that right?"

Avery was a quick learner and nodded enthusiastically. "Yep. That's the very honest truth."

She looked so sincere that Courtney almost believed her, and she knew it was a lie. Poor Richard would have his hands full with this little girl when she reached puberty.

Principal Cain scowled, but Courtney could see the wheels churning. If she had to call social services, that would be at least an hour added to her day. If they waited for Richard, that would be more.

"We'll see you two tomorrow," Principal Cain said and walked inside the building.

Courtney made a mental note to herself to make sure she was never late again, and she was to make certain Jesse's emergency directions were to let no one but family take her son home.

She handed each kid a cookie and walked them to her beat-up Jeep. As soon as they were inside, she asked Avery what her father's phone number was. She was proud of both Richard and Avery. Richard for making sure she had it memorized and Avery for remembering it.

She dialed and got his voice mail.

"Richard, this is Courtney Sweet. It seems our paths cross again. Whoever you entrusted to pick up Avery was a no-show. I've got her, so don't worry. I'll make sure her homework is done, and she gets fed. You know where to find us."

She turned to look at the two of them eating their cookies in the back seat.

"Here are the rules for the day." She smiled. "When we get home, you get thirty minutes of cartoons to unwind. There will be no rock throwing. Next is homework and then dinner, and if there's time, I'm going to whoop you both at Candy Land."

In the rearview mirror, Courtney watched the two try not to smile.

"Is your mother for real?"

Jesse laughed. "Shh, I don't know who picked us up, but it's not my mother."

They went back and forth, talking about alien abduction until Courtney was laughing.

Had she been so busy trying to make a living that she forgot how to live?

CHAPTER SIX

Richard sat in the terminal staring at his phone and replaying the message he'd received from Principal Cain. Avery had not been picked up. He immediately called Britney, the after-school babysitter. She was a college kid who needed extra cash but obviously was financially pat today. When he asked why she didn't show up, her answer stunned him. She didn't feel like it.

Well, his daughter didn't feel like going to school, but he made her. She didn't like spinach, but she ate it because it was good for her. He didn't like doing lots of things, like these short commuter flights, but he did them because he had a child and a mortgage and all the stuff that came with being an adult.

His phone pinged with incoming messages that took him several minutes to get through. The last one stunned him. Courtney called to say she had his daughter.

He didn't know how that transpired, but he was grateful she stepped in and helped out. He needed a backup plan. College kids couldn't be his long-term solution. They were still adults in training. On most days, his ten-year-old had more common sense than half the hires he'd gone through.

One sitter thought cereal for dinner was nutritious because Captain Crunch had crunch berries, and a berry was fruit. Another thought a frat party was an excellent socialization exercise for Avery. It took him forever to explain the difference between a beer bong and beer pong. Both were inappropriate for a child of Avery's age at the time—nine.

He dialed Courtney's number before he boarded the flight to Aspen, but didn't get an answer. He calmed his racing heart by reminding himself that while Courtney wasn't part of his fan club, she was a parent and had raised a boy on her own. Jesse seemed like a good kid—reasonably good, anyway. He lost points for the rock incident, but Richard remembered a young girl named Tabatha Ryker who grabbed his shirt when he was Jesse's age. She tugged so hard it split the seams, and all because she had a crush on him. He closed his eyes and thought about Avery as a teen and decided he wasn't ready for that.

There was a specific skill set required to raise girls, which he lacked in so many ways. He read *A Survival Guide for Single Fathers of Tween and Teen Daughters*. That only solidified his belief that he was in for a wild ride. Fathers couldn't keep their daughters little forever, no matter how appealing that seemed. Avery would grow up and push all his buttons. He'd probably be gray or bald in a decade.

When it came time for the crew to board the plane, he entered the cockpit and started precheck.

His copilot's name was Greg. The regional flights didn't pay as well as the long-haul flights, but they were a good way for pilots like Greg, who flew longer legs, to get more hours in between international flights.

KELLY COLLINS

"Why is there always glitter in the cockpit?" Greg brushed his seat, but the glitter was embedded.

"Pink glitter is my color," Richard teased. "Have you not looked at me? I have a daughter, and glitter comes in everything from lotion to crayons these days. You can't get away from it. If they did a DNA test, one component of Avery would be glitter."

Greg whistled. "I don't know how you do it."

Richard took a moment to count all his shortcomings. "Poorly."

After system checks, they took off toward Aspen. With a fifty-minute flight time and a thirty-minute drive, he was looking at getting to Courtney's close to six thirty.

He hated this job, but it paid the bills.

"Rumor has it they are realigning the flights and there are big changes coming."

"There's always speculation." That had been the rumor for the last three years, but it never happened. He wasn't worried.

"Something has to change. These short flights aren't profitable."

"Pricier flights compensate for the less profitable ones."

They hit a little turbulence as expected in the mountains but landed safely in Aspen.

Greg nodded toward the small flight school in the distance.

"Could you imagine owning that?"

Richard looked to where Altitude Flight School sat.

"That was my dream."

Greg went through the post-flight checks as if on autopilot.

"You want to teach flying and pull banners around to make ends meet?"

He took another glance at the biplane taking off with an aerial ad that said, "Always choose love."

"Wouldn't that be great? I mean, your world, your rules, right?"

"Pay sucks and if you do a crap job of advertising, there is no pay."

"You sound like my late wife." Cadence put a kibosh on his dream of owning a flight school right away. She didn't want to depend on his ability to keep students. She didn't want lean months in the winter and long hours in the summer. All she wanted were spa days and vacays. Those were her exact words.

"Hey man, I'm sorry about your loss."

Most of the time, no one said a thing, and Richard liked it that way. "I'm sorry" was the polite thing to say, and his response was always, "Life and death happen."

"Yeah, but wow, losing your wife had to be hard."

Again, he gave the standard reply. "Life is hard."

They gathered their things and left the cockpit. He rushed out of the airport and drove to 333 Witches Coven Way in Timberline. As he passed the surrounding streets, he saw names like Broomstick Drive and Hocus Pocus Lane. Some developer had a field day naming this area of town they called Happy Hollow.

He pulled into the driveway and hurried to the door. Before he could knock, Jesse opened it.

"Mom says to come in."

"How did you know I was here?"

He pointed to the fancy doorbell that recorded visitors. "It makes noise when someone comes to the door. Mom has an app and can see what's going on."

He stepped inside and was greeted with the smell of garlic and spices. It was like walking into Little Italy, a small Italian restaurant in Aspen by Luxe Resorts.

"Smells amazing." His stomach growled so loud he was sure anyone within half a mile could hear it.

"Come in," Courtney said from the kitchen. She peeked around the corner and smiled. "Wow, nice uniform."

47

He straightened his tie and walked forward. On a typical day, he would have taken it off by now, but he had rushed over and didn't think about it. Then again, maybe somewhere in the back of his mind, he wanted to look respectable. He wasn't an irresponsible parent and hoped that his professional attire would help steer her opinion of him to the good. He already made several wrong impressions when it came to Courtney. He could and would do better.

"I'm sorry this happened." He looked at Courtney and then at Avery, who stood next to her buttering garlic bread. "I had it under control."

Courtney raised a brow, but it wasn't a move that made him feel like she was judging him. She was calling him on his bullshit.

"Life happens." She nodded to the empty chair at the island. "Take a seat. Dinner is almost ready."

He sat but shook his head. "Oh, no. I should get Avery and be out of your hair."

"No way, Daddy. We're staying. I helped make the pasta."

Avery was a stubborn one, but she rarely demanded anything. His stomach grumbled again.

"Sounds like your stomach says yes," Jesse said.

He was a little embarrassed by the ravenous lion sound it was making. Today he flew from Aspen to Denver and back twice, and only had time for a coffee, a protein bar, and a couple bags of pretzels.

"I could eat." He breathed in what smelled like oregano and tomatoes. "What kind did you make?"

"We didn't open a box and boil it. We made it from scratch and put it through a machine. Jesse's favorite is spaghetti, so we made that."

He turned to Jesse, who was blond like his mom, but he didn't have her eyes. His were more green than blue.

"That's my favorite too. Although, I love a good lasagna."

Courtney slid the buttered garlic bread into the oven and drained the pan of pasta that sat on the stovetop.

"I make a killer lasagna too."

"I can't wait to taste it." He chuckled. "I mean the spaghetti. I'd never invite myself over for lasagna."

She poured a glass of red wine and offered it to him. He debated on whether to drink it and decided one glass would be fine.

"Thank you." He took a sip and savored the robust flavor of what could only be Chianti with its rounded straw-covered bottle. "This is so good."

"I get it at the little Italian store attached to Little Italy. Do you know the place?"

He let out a hum. "Know it. Love it."

She gave Jesse a look, and he seemed to know that she wanted him to set the table. He and Avery hustled to get everything in place before the bread came out of the oven.

"You'll have to teach me that look. Do you think it would work in the clean your room department? Or what about going to bed?"

She laughed, and it was a sweet sound. "I've got completely different looks for those. I'll teach you them."

Being here felt so comfortable. He looked around to make sure Avery wasn't within listening range.

"I'm truly sorry for what happened. I was in flight when the principal called."

"What happened to Britney?"

He groaned and rubbed his palm over his five-o'clock shadow.

"Do you have a week? I swear she was probably dropped on her head at birth."

"Is she okay?"

He stared at her, not knowing exactly what she was asking. "The dropping at birth or why she didn't show up?"

Courtney turned around and bent over to take the bread from the oven. Today she was in nice-fitting jeans, and they looked damn fine on her. When she turned back with the bread pan in her hand and a smirk on her face, he knew he'd been caught staring.

"How old is this Britney?"

He scrunched his nose and pursed his lips. "Twenty going on nine, I'd say."

Courtney shook her head. "Good help is hard to find. I had a teenage babysitter once that allowed Jesse to repaint his bedroom while I was gone. That included his bedding and the carpet. That was when I realized no one could ever look after him like I do."

"You're lucky you have the kind of job that allows you to stay with him."

She tossed the pasta into a bowl and mixed in a bit of sauce.

"I had to make a choice a long time ago. Jesse didn't ask to come into this world, so I owed him my best when I brought him into it. My best doesn't mean we have everything we want, but we have what we need."

She handed him the bowl of pasta, and she picked up the sauce and garlic bread.

"Let's eat," she called out to the kids, who were in the living room playing checkers.

She set the food down and went back for a salad she had in the refrigerator. On her way back, she grabbed their glasses of wine.

"So, what happened to Britney?"

He took the empty seat after Courtney, and the kids took theirs. "Oh, you know. She wasn't feeling it today."

She passed the bowls, and everyone served themselves. Jesse waited and as soon as everyone was done, they held hands, and he said grace. It was a simple "thank you for our food, our blessings, and our friends" kind of thing.

Richard took his first bite and let the flavors dance across his taste buds. There was garlic and tomato and oregano and cheese.

"Better than Little Italy."

Courtney blushed. "But they're the best."

"They used to be."

She bowed her head and whispered, "Thank you."

They ate as the kids chatted about an upcoming science project.

He stared at the woman beside him. She was sassy, sweet, spicy, and all things in between.

"Do you fly tomorrow?"

He was so worried about today that he hadn't thought about tomorrow or making plans for Avery.

"I do." He sighed deeply.

"Is Britney on board?"

"Doesn't matter. I can't risk another day with Principal Cain breathing down my back. I'll have to call out and make arrangements." The options were limited to after-school programs that didn't have the flexibility he needed or too-expensive centers that weren't open on weekends.

She twirled the spaghetti around her fork. "How about we make a deal?"

It was his turn to raise a brow. "I'm listening."

"I really can't afford the dentist bill, and you can't afford to have Avery left at school, so what if I work off the debt?"

"You want to work for me?"

CHAPTER SEVEN

Courtney stared at him for a few seconds.

"No, I don't want to work for you, but it seems like a logical solution to both of our problems. I can't afford another bill, and you can't afford to have Avery neglected."

She hated to put it that way, but when his daughter was left at school with no alternatives, that could only be considered neglect. At least that was what the court system would think, and she didn't want to see that happen.

It was obvious he loved his daughter. They had both been through a terrible experience. He had lost his wife and Avery her mother. It would be a shame to have them lose each other next.

"I thought you owned the bakery."

She wiped her mouth with her napkin. "I do."

He gave her an I-don't-believe-you look. "That's not the exact story your brother gave me."

She pursed her lips, then drew them into a thin line.

Most of the time she loved her brother, but there were times she wanted to dislike him very much. This was one of those times.

While it was true, she didn't own the bakery out and out, she owned a bit of it. Saying that she owned it made her feel better about herself. Being the owner of something sounded better than saying that I keep the books.

"Okay, I don't exactly own it. It's a family bakery and, in truth, I own the smallest fraction." She glanced at the kids who were paying the grownups no mind. "I probably own the equivalent of an oven, and not the new oven Chloe installed recently, but the one that came with the building in 1950 and is now sitting in the alley awaiting disposal."

"So, you fibbed." He smiled. "I'm not sure I want someone who so easily bends the truth to be an influence over my daughter."

She gasped. "No? You'd rather have someone who sits on her brains all day teach her how to be a good human?" She leaned in close enough to smell his cologne. It was something spicy like cinnamon and vanilla. "I bet you didn't hire her for her brains."

His eyes widened. "You're not implying that I hired her for other reasons, are you?" He picked up his glass of wine and finished it, setting the glass aside. "I'm not looking for any of that. I can barely keep my head above water as it is. My schedule stinks. It's easier to buy new clothes than wash them. We eat take out most nights of the week. I'm failing at everything." He scrubbed his face with his palms. "My doctor tells me if I don't get my blood pressure down, I'm going to be in trouble."

The conversation was quickly getting to the place where they were likely to pick up stones and lob them at each other.

Her ego was bruised because she felt inadequate. His life was a mess because it was overwhelming. They were both failing but for different reasons.

She rose from the table.

"How about some cookies?" That got the kids' attention.

"I'll get them," Jesse called.

"I'll help."

They both picked up their empty plates and placed them in the sink.

Richard looked at her with confusion. "How did you do that?"

"Do what?" She cocked her head.

"Get them to clear their plates from the table."

She laughed and shrugged. "I suppose I set an expectation for Jesse, and he follows through so he doesn't disappoint me. Kids want to please you, but they also have a herd mentality. They will do what the other kids are doing. I imagine Avery was just following along."

"It can't be that easy."

She shook her head. "No, it's not." She nodded toward Jesse. "That is eleven years in the making."

"He's eleven?"

Technically, he was still ten, but his birthday was fast approaching.

"Almost."

"Another fib?" he teased.

She lifted her chin. "An embellishment of the truth."

"Which is still a fib."

"Yes." She let her shoulders slump. "It's a fib."

Jesse brought back the container of cookies and a few napkins. "Can we eat ours in the living room? We want to finish our game before Avery has to go."

Courtney opened the container and placed a cookie on each napkin before shooing the kids toward their game.

"How did they go from bitter enemies to best friends in a day?" Courtney asked.

He smiled, and boy did that smile do something to her insides.

They twisted and turned but not in the belly ache kind of way. It was the warm-inside churning that heated up all her bits.

She picked up her glass of wine and finished it, trying to distract herself from the hot devil in the pilot's uniform in front of her.

"You and I both know they were never bitter enemies."

She giggled. "That's true." She felt bad for what she'd said. "Listen, I didn't mean to imply that you hired Britney for anything but her..." She tried to pick her words carefully. "Her flexible schedule. It came out wrong, and I apologize for putting you on the defensive."

He took a bite of cookie. Even the way he chewed was sexy. Some men ate with their mouths open, which took all the sexiness out of the eating process. No one wanted to see chewed up food in someone else's mouth. Richard ate with his eyes, too. She could see how much he enjoyed the sweetness of the treat by the way the gold speckles in his blue eyes seemed to dance.

"I apologize as well. Criticism isn't something I take lightly. It's like picking at a scab from an old wound."

She wondered if his wife was often critical of him but didn't feel it was her place to ask.

"How about we start over again?"

He set down his cookie.

"Hi, I'm Richard Shipton. Don't confuse me with my alter ego, Dick Shipton, who has shown up more than I'd have liked in the last couple of days."

The laugh started in her shoulders and rolled through her like an earthquake until she couldn't stop shaking. She laughed so hard she snorted, which made him laugh with her.

When they finished, she was nearly crying. It had been a long time since she'd laughed that hard, and it felt good. There was a drunken feeling that came from pure joy. It was better than any glass of wine could offer.

"Nice to meet you, Richard. I'm Courtney. I hear you're looking for someone to look after your daughter when you're working."

He sat up and replaced his smile with a serious look.

"Is this an interview?"

She looked down at her jeans and T-shirt. "I'd normally dress better for an interview or at least I'd think I would. I've never been interviewed for a job before."

He sat back, causing the chair to creak, but she knew it wouldn't break. The table and chairs had belonged to her grandparents and had been passed on from generation to generation. If it survived her father and her brother, it would certainly survive Richard.

"I like the jeans." The corners of his lips lifted slightly before his serious expression fell into place again.

"It's my preferred uniform," she teased. "A mom has to be ready for anything from Kool-Aid spills to throw up."

He stared at her for a moment, and she felt like she was under a magnifying glass.

"How do you feel about glitter?"

She relaxed. "I don't have much recent experience with glitter, but I'm willing to try new things. I think it's important to open your life to fresh experiences." The last time she'd played with glitter was when she embellished Gage's shoelaces. He was about sixteen, and she slathered them with white glue and dipped them into iridescent glitter. Her brother wasn't happy, but she thought it gave his plain Chucks that little something extra.

"Can you braid hair?"

She pulled her hair to the side and whipped up a quick braid. "I don't have my resume ready, but I can French braid, do a fish-

A LAYER OF LOVE

tail, and I'm great with ponytails. Give me a few hair ties and a brush and I can blow your mind."

He seemed to be enjoying this "interview" and so was she. It was light and airy and, in truth, nice to have another adult in the room. When she went to the early morning meetup, she wasn't trying to hook up. She just wanted to feel like a grown-up again.

"I don't want to saddle you with my problems."

She tapped her fingers on the table. "First, Avery is not a problem. The problem is things cost too much money and people have to work. It's a vicious cycle. We want to eat and need money for food. Kids grow fast and need clothes. Clothes cost money. We have to put a roof over our heads because it gets cold at night in the mountains. We just need a plan."

He nodded. "I really can't thank you enough for picking her up."

She almost forgot to tell him. "I fibbed to Principal Cain. She was ready to call someone to get Avery, and I told her that you and I had made arrangements the night before. Shame on you ... you forgot to call and tell her to update Avery's emergency contacts."

"You are quite the fibber, aren't you?"

She bit her lip and let it pop loose. "I'm normally not, but you seem to bring the worst out in me." She held a finger up. "In this case, it worked out in your favor."

He held up a finger, too. "And it seems that the good deed will work in your favor as well because I am willing to forget the dental bill for your kindness."

She shook her head. "Oh no. I want to pay it." She groaned. "I mean, I don't want to pay it, but I agree that it's my responsibility as Jesse's mom to cover the cost that your insurance doesn't. Besides, you made a big point of handing me the bill, so it's obviously important to you."

He rubbed at his chin, and she heard the sandpapery scruff under his fingertips.

"It was the principle of the situation. Like we said, we got off to a bad start. You were like a stone in my shoe, and no matter how hard I tried, I couldn't shake you loose."

She slid her chair back a few inches. "That's not flattering."

"No, it's not, but that's why we started again. As far as Avery, I'd love it if you could take over for Britney. I'm sure you could do a far better job."

"You're not setting the bar high. All I have to do is show up and that's a given since our children are in the same class."

"I would really appreciate your help, but I insist on paying you for your time."

She looked to the ceiling. "I'll work off the debt, and then we'll go from there."

He offered his hand to shake. "That's a deal. What's your hourly rate?"

She rose from the table, taking their dishes with her. "Oh, you can't afford me, but I'm looking forward to the time when you owe me."

CHAPTER EIGHT

The last few days had been absolute bliss for Richard. He didn't have to worry if Avery was picked up because he knew Courtney had her. And by the time he arrived to get her, homework was done, and she was always fed and happy. He was happy too. Happier than he had a right to be.

Courtney often packed a meal for him that was on the counter waiting for his arrival. All he had to do was put it in the microwave when he got home. He found himself reflecting on his life. There was the time before Courtney and after Courtney. It used to be that when he got home, he and Avery ate and fought about home-work and bedtime. These days, he had quality time to spend with her. She was a wicked checkers player, and they started reading *The One and Only Ivan,* a book about a gorilla who spends his life as an attraction in a shopping mall.

The story was a wake-up call for him as well. He'd been like Ivan and lived the life the world thrust upon him, but after meeting Courtney, he realized that maybe his life wasn't all it could be.

He was still behind in laundry, but with Courtney's help, his daughter was no longer a mixed-up mess, because she sewed in tags that said what color the garment was and also wrote him a cheat sheet that outlined acceptable color combinations.

As for him, his wardrobe consisted of various shades of blue. He figured he couldn't go wrong with that. Mostly, he wore his uniform, which was blue and had a sprinkling of glitter that seemed to match everything.

He and his copilot Greg were paired up again, which was fine by Richard. Greg was efficient and wasn't all that chatty.

"Things good at home?" Greg asked, and he throttled the engine back and powered down the plane.

Well, he didn't use to be chatty.

"Everything is great. Why do you ask?"

The man shrugged as he stood and walked to unlock the cockpit door.

"I don't know. You seem different ... At peace."

He felt at peace but didn't know it showed.

"I got Avery's after school care worked out. That takes a lot of pressure off me."

Greg swiped his pants. "But we still have a glitter issue."

Richard smiled. "Only a problem if you don't like glitter."

They stood by the door and waved and smiled as the passengers exited.

"Is she hot?" Greg asked.

Richard leaned against the door. "Is who hot?"

"The babysitter."

"She's a mom." Not that he had a problem with moms. He just wanted to shut down where this conversation was going and fast. He wasn't comfortable talking about Courtney to Greg. It was odd, but he kind of wanted to keep her to himself.

"Okay then, is she a mom you'd like to—"

"I'm not talking about her." As the last passenger exited, the crew filed out after. "All I'll say is she's responsible, she's a great cook, and my daughter likes her."

"Good, that's a start. You can't stay single forever. Eventually you'll have to let someone in to fill all the empty spaces your wife left behind."

He was certain Greg was referring to what a loving wife would leave behind, but Cadence left destruction in her path and a lot of unanswered questions in her wake.

They walked down the terminal and went their separate ways in the parking lot.

When he thought of Cadence, he didn't think of the hollow voids she'd left behind with her death. He remembered the emptiness he felt when she was alive. How was it possible to live with someone and feel so alone?

How crazy was it that the minutes he spent with Courtney were far more satisfying than the years he'd spent with his wife?

It used to be that his favorite part of the day was climbing into the cockpit, but not anymore. His favorite time was the moment he pulled into the Sweets' driveway, and Avery bounded out of the house and threw herself into his arms. Equally favorite was when he walked inside the house to smell whatever Courtney had cooked. She always had a sweet greeting and a soft smile for him.

This was how he'd dreamed his marriage would be. Instead, he often came home to a babysitter and an excuse as to why Cadence wasn't home.

It was a thirty-minute commute from work to happiness, and just like yesterday, the door flew open, and Avery ran outside. She'd only be toothless for one more day. Her flipper was in, and they would pick it up tomorrow on his day off.

Since Courtney had been so great about feeding all of them, he thought he'd return the favor and take them out to eat tomorrow night.

"Daddy!"

Avery ran into his arms, and he picked her up and swung her around in a circle.

"Hey, little bird. How are you?"

She rambled on at Mach speed. "We're baking."

"You are?" These were the things he appreciated. Though men could bake, he never had, and so baking wasn't something he could teach Avery.

"Yes." She slid to the ground and took his hand, pulling him into the house. "Daddy's home," she called out to everyone within listening distance.

Courtney laughed. "Welcome home, dear," she teased. "How was your day?" It was a very fifties-era sitcom thing to say, and she meant it to be funny, so he laughed, but if he were telling the truth, he liked coming home to a houseful of happy people.

"Hey, sport," he said to Jesse, ruffling his hair as he walked by.

"Hey," he said in a lowered, dejected-sounding voice.

"What's up, kiddo?"

Jesse frowned. "The math homework is hard, and Mom won't let me copy Avery's paper."

He looked at Courtney, who shrugged and said, "It's the rules. I asked him if he needed my help, but he said the last time I helped he didn't do well."

Richard laughed. "Your mom is an accountant. If anyone can do math, it's probably her."

"Bookkeeper," Courtney corrected. "I never went to college."

"But you're qualified to do fifth grade math, I'm sure." He pointed to the chair. "Do you mind if I sit?" He looked at the ingredients laid out on the island in front of the girls. "It looks like you're in the middle of something."

Courtney smiled. "Sit. Make yourself at home. Can I get you coffee? Wine? Soda?"

"I'd love a soda."

She pivoted toward the refrigerator and took out a soda before getting a glass and filling it with ice.

"I've got a chicken in the oven. Avery and I thought we'd give this *Recipe for Love* book a try." She winked. "Don't worry, Dad, she's not picking out wedding gowns and flowers. We figured we'd focus on self-love."

Perspective. That's what opening his life up to others has offered him.

"Self-love is good. While you do that, can I help Jesse with his homework? I've got some math skills of my own."

"I'm sure he'd love that. Since you're here, and I'm late with dinner, maybe you can stay and eat with us?"

Did he hear hope in her voice?

"I wouldn't want to be anywhere else." That was the truth. In a short time, Courtney Sweet had knocked him off balance, but he liked the way it felt. It was kind of like being drunk without the hangover.

He sat with Jesse.

"I just don't understand fractions. Why, when I'm multiplying, I can just multiply across, but when I'm dividing, I have to turn it into a multiplication problem and flip the second number so the denominator is now the top and the numerator is the bottom."

Richard looked at Courtney, who was watching to see how he'd answer. He smiled and told Jesse, "Fractions are like women. They're complicated, but once you understand the rules, you can figure out the problem."

Jesse sighed. "But it always seems like once I learn something new, the rules change."

"I feel your pain, son. I really do, but this is easy—easier than girls, anyway."

"Hey, we may be complicated, but we're worth it," Courtney said.

While Jesse dug into his math homework, Richard watched his daughter thrive under Courtney's attention.

"What should we make?" Courtney asked. "I read the preface and it said that we can choose the recipe ourselves, or we can let the book choose for us."

Avery looked at the *Recipes for Love* book and set it on the counter. "Let's live on the edge and let the book choose."

"You raised a little daredevil."

He sipped his soda and set it down. "Don't remind me."

Courtney put her thumb at the end of the book. "Okay, I'll let the pages fall, and you say stop when you think we've reached the recipe that's meant for us. Okay?"

Avery nodded enthusiastically while Courtney thumbed through the book.

"Stop," she said.

When Courtney opened the book, it was on a page called A Layer of Love Cake.

"Is that what we're making?" Avery asked.

"We have to follow the rules, and they say pick one recipe and only one. So this is it."

Avery looked at him. "Daddy, do you think you can learn about love from a cookbook?"

CHAPTER NINE

Courtney watched Richard to see how he'd answer his daughter. She didn't know much about his relationship with his wife, but she'd picked up enough to know they'd had their problems.

She wasn't naïve when it came to love. No relationship was perfect. She imagined it was like a math problem. You had to approach it open-minded and with a plan. First, you had to know what the problem was and then identify the facts. Then you figured out what it was asking for and you eliminated the excess information or noise. It was important to pay attention to the details. Once you had done all that, you could find a solution. If you couldn't, it was time to seek help. The problem with relationships and math was that no one wanted to do the hard work.

"I think you can learn about love from everything around you. The lessons out there aren't only about how to love, but sometimes they also teach you how you shouldn't love. Let's see what this recipe teaches you."

It was a diplomatic response, and she had to applaud him for steering his daughter into exploring all the information before she made a decision.

"Let's make sure we've got what we need." They read through the ingredients and laid them on the counter in order of use.

While she was never the baker in the family business, she learned a lot by watching. Her father was always meticulous in the way he approached his day. He'd set out everything he needed because it saved time and headaches.

"Shall we read what Adelaide Phelps has to say about her layer cake?" She pointed to the page. "Why don't you read it for me. Let me know if you need help with any of the words."

Avery smiled like she'd been given the lead part in the school play.

Dear Baker,

Over the years, I've learned a lot about love. If you listen to the Greeks, they'll tell you there are eight kinds of love.

Passionate (Eros)

Enduring (Pragma)

Playful (Ludus)

Universal (Agape)

Deep friendship (Philia)

Self-love (Philautia)

Familial love (Storge)

Obsessive love (Mania)

I don't know nothing about Greek philosophy, but I know about love, and it's pretty simple. It all comes from the same place—your heart. You get into trouble with love when you let your mind have a bigger role than your heart.

As I sat down to write this recipe, I considered all the Greek kinds of love and realized I'd experienced them all.

My Sam was the Eros kind of love—passionate. But our love was also Pragma and Ludus and Storge and Philia—enduring, play-

ful, and familial once we added Sam Junior. But you can't really have love without friendship first. Together we created an Agape kind of love that was universal and was the cornerstone to how we lived our lives. That leaves Philautia and Mania, which to me means that no one can truly love you until you learn to love yourself. As for Mania, who isn't a little obsessive when it comes to love? Love is like chocolate: you never really have enough to quench the cravings.

Back to the layers of love, though. No matter what kind of love you think you have, like a decadent cake, it's built with layers. This is the one thing I know to be true.

The first layer of love is the beginning of everything. In this cake, it's the first thing you'll put down. Some would call it attraction, but I'd call it flavor. For this cake, it can be any of a rainbow of colors and flavors, but you may want to choose chocolate or spice. We like what we like.

That second layer goes a little deeper. It's not the first hello anymore. We're building something more, so we add on another layer, which adds depth. For a relationship, it might mean getting to know them better. There's nothing worse than being with someone who doesn't make you feel anything.

Avery stopped reading and looked at Courtney. "Are we baking a cake or is she telling a story?"

That was a good question. "I think it's both." She pointed to the cookbook. "I imagine Adelaide Phelps was a wise woman who worked out a lot of her problems by baking. I love the way she is telling us in a fun way that love is simple, and yet, like a cake, you have to create it carefully. Go on." She leaned on the counter and waited for Avery to continue. Courtney's eyes drifted to Richard and found that he was as interested in the story as she was. Jesse, on the other hand, was furiously finishing his homework.

Layer three is the core. It's a big commitment to make a five-

layer cake. As you stack the layers on top of each other, nothing will work if the foundation isn't solid. In love, this is where you find out the true ingredients of a person. What are their dreams and aspirations? Are they made from the same stuff you are? Remember that quality ingredients are important but mixing quality salt and quality sugar isn't going to taste as sweet. Compatibility is the key.

One day my son Sam brought home a girl named Freya Gunther. She was a nice girl, but not "the" girl. I knew it because I could see that Freya was honey and my boy was sugar. One would think that sugar and honey would mix well since they're both sweet, but in my experience all that sweet will do is give you a bellyache and rotten teeth. One day Sam brought home Deborah. Now Deborah wasn't a pushover. That girl had some spice to her and mixed beautifully with Sam's sweetness. Too much of one thing is never good, so measure your ingredients wisely.

The fourth layer is when this cake gets serious. It's also the layer of love that requires a commitment. Once you stack it, there's no going back, so it's the promise layer. It's the almost-there layer. It's where you decide you're all in because no one makes a four-layer cake. This is where you carefully place more on the foundation you've built, because if you've done it right, there's no worry about it toppling over. If you've done it right, it's staying in place.

The fifth layer is where all the good stuff comes together. It's where you put the icing on and maybe some sprinkles, and you celebrate the accomplishment because you've built the layers from the ground up. You've added the flavor that appeals to you and now you can enjoy its sweetness.

Anyway, the point of this recipe is to show that love, no matter what kind of love, comes from the heart. Anything that comes from your heart is worth the effort. Put in the time and make sure to use quality ingredients and you can't go wrong. The important thing for both the cake and love is to build a strong foundation.

"Aww, that is so sweet." She was moved by the woman's recipe. They were making a basic vanilla cake recipe, but it was so much more. "It makes me want to read all the other recipes. She's like the grandma you wished you had."

Avery frowned. "I don't have a grandma."

"No?" Courtney looked at Richard.

"Both my parents and Cadence's parents have passed."

Jesse lifted his head.

"I'll share mine with you. She makes the best cookies." His eyes grew wide. "I mean the second best. Mom's cookies are always the best."

Courtney walked around and kissed her son on the head. "Now that's some sugar."

"All you need is spice and you've got a recipe for love," Avery said.

While the girls mixed up the batter and poured it into the pans, the boys set the table. Courtney felt happier than she had in a long time. Happier than she had a right to.

If she had to describe domestic bliss, this would have been it. Two kids not fighting, a man who wasn't afraid to help in the kitchen, and a good meal to share. This was almost enough. Almost because there were things she missed like holding hands and kissing and snuggling up to a warm body when it was cold outside.

She was young when she got pregnant. She hardly had her adult brains, but Adelaide was right. A relationship was built from the ground up and she and Jesse's dad started somewhere around layer five. They went straight for the sprinkles—the good stuff— and it was the good stuff that left her pregnant and alone.

As soon as the chicken came out of the oven, the cakes went in. They gathered around the table like they'd done it a hundred times before. It all felt so natural.

"I don't think we'll have time to cool the cake and decorate, so why don't we plan to do that tomorrow?" But then she remembered Avery wouldn't be there, and her heart ached. "Oh, you won't be here." She smiled, happy that Avery would get her teeth but sad that a part of what had come to feel like family would be missing. "What if you come over for dinner anyway? And we can decorate the cake and celebrate your smile."

Richard held up his hand. "I almost forgot. Avery and I would like to invite you and Jesse out to dinner tomorrow night. You've been cooking for us all week and it's our turn to take care of you."

Jesse laughed. "Are you asking my mom on a date?"

All eyes went to Richard, who seemed to be at a loss for words.

"Jesse, he's asking us both to dinner. Not a date but a celebration for Avery, who will have her beautiful smile restored."

She could see the relief on Richard's face when she chimed in. The thought of a date sounded nice, though. She hadn't been on one since she was in her twenties, but she understood what this was. It was an arrangement. They weren't a couple. They were two people who needed something from each other. But what if what they needed was love? If they were a cake, what layer would they be on?

CHAPTER TEN

"Smile for me," Richard said.

Avery smiled broadly to show off her new teeth. She'd been so brave about it all, but that was who his little girl was. She was a soldier who'd walked across several battlefields and come out a victor.

"Do I look pretty?"

"I thought you were pretty without teeth too." He touched her nose with his finger. A little bop that made her giggle. "Remember that beauty comes from inside. Sometimes the people who are prettiest on the outside aren't always so lovely on the inside." It was a concept that she'd learn over time. Most people, given a choice between taking a shiny new penny or a tarnished coin, would choose the shiny one. It sparkled and looked nice, but the smart people would look deeper at the coin to see its value. A new penny was almost worthless, whereas a tarnished coin could be old and valuable. It was when you looked deeper that you found the true treasure.

"Do you think Ms. Sweet is pretty?"

He was a wise man, and this was a trick question. If he said yes, Avery would want to know if she was prettier than her, and if he said no, she'd wonder why he wasn't looking deeper.

Courtney was gorgeous. What made her even prettier was that he was pretty sure she didn't know how beautiful she truly was.

"Why do you ask?"

Avery smiled. "Because I think she's pretty."

"I'd say you have a good eye for beauty."

The dentist gave them all the directions and warnings that go with retainers and sent them on their way.

"Can we go over to Jesse's right now?"

He checked his watch and saw it was three thirty. "It's still too early. We said we'd show up at five. It's not polite to arrive too early."

She fisted her hips and gave him a stern look. "Daddy, you tell me the early bird gets the worm."

"That's for something different. We're not after worms."

"You can't change the rules."

He had to give her credit for her argument. "You'd make a good lawyer."

"No, I'm going to be a teacher."

He ruffled her hair. "You'll be good at that too." She was already a good teacher. He had to admit that he probably learned more from her than he could ever teach her.

"Can you call and ask? I want to decorate the love cake."

They got in the car, and he pulled out his phone because if he said no, she'd only tell him that those who don't ask don't get. It was a lesson he told her often. There was no harm in asking. The worst that could happen was the person said no, and then there would be no guessing.

The phone rang once before Courtney said hello.

"Hey, Courtney. I've got an antsy beauty queen that wants to show off her new smile and frost a cake. Are you up for early visitors?" He didn't wait for her answer before adding, "Feel free to say no. I realize I've caught you off guard."

"Come on over. We're finishing up homework. Tell Avery that Jesse got her assignments."

"Oh, she'll love that," he said with a dose of sarcasm. "We'll see you in a few minutes."

Avery smiled brightly like she'd won a prize. "See, Daddy, you never know until you ask."

"You're right." He put the car in drive and turned toward the west side of town. "Jesse picked up your homework for you."

His daughter growled. "I hate that boy."

"No, you don't."

She huffed. "I do. He's supposed to be my friend. What friend brings you schoolwork?"

"The kind who doesn't want you to get behind."

"Fine. Can we get flowers for Ms. Sweet?"

He narrowed his eyes. Although she was half his, she also had her mother's manipulative gene.

"Is this really about flowers or delaying the dreaded homework?"

Her delay told him the truth.

"Flowers some other day, then." It's not that flowers were a bad idea, but they sent a message—a message he wasn't sure he wanted out there.

There was so much to consider when opening his life to another woman. Cadence had been gone for years, but her betrayal still felt raw and painful.

He pulled into the driveway and took a deep breath. He would need it because each time he saw Courtney, she took the air from his lungs.

KELLY COLLINS

The door flew open, and this time it was Jesse who ran out and opened Avery's door. "I set up the checkerboard. Let's go."

In the doorway, leaning against the doorjamb, was Courtney. Today she wore a light-blue sundress and sandals. Her hair was pulled back in a decorative barrette.

"Hey, stranger, come on inside. I've just made a pot of coffee."

He followed her inside the house. Only today, it didn't smell like dinner. It smelled like something sweet.

"Avery," Courtney called out. "While you play checkers with Jesse, do you mind if your dad helps frost the cake, and then you and Jesse can use the sprinkles to make it pretty?"

Avery looked at the cake and then at the checkers. It was apparent that she was torn, but then Jesse told her that the sprinkles were the fun part, and she abandoned the idea of the icing.

"Looks like it's you and me. Are you up for something sweet?"

He could take that all kinds of ways. When he looked at her, it didn't seem like she was talking strictly about icing a cake, either.

"Should we pull out the book?"

She grabbed it and handed it to him.

"You can look at the recipe, but I've already read it, and it says something about everything on the outside being superficial. It's the inside that makes it worth a taste."

He chuckled, remembering his earlier conversation with Avery about the same concept.

He set his hand on the cover, over the heart. Was it possible to feel the beat of an old book?

"I made some buttercream frosting from the recipe." She leaned in close enough for him to smell her perfume. It was a mix of something sweet like vanilla and a dash of floral. He breathed in deeply and pinpointed the flower to pikake, a common flower used in Hawaiian leis.

He closed his eyes and pictured Cadence standing on the

74

balcony of their villa in Maui with a lei around her neck. It was the only time his job was agreeable with her because they got free flights for their honeymoon.

"What did the first layer represent?" he asked.

She pushed the icing his way and put the first layer on a plate. It wasn't a fancy pedestal dish like his wife would have used. This was a simple plate with a chip on the side.

"Adelaide Phelps would say it was the beginning. You need to set a strong foundation to build upon."

"That's right, I remember."

She slid a flat metal spatula in his direction. "Put a thin, even layer only on the top. We'll frost the sides later."

He did as she said. With each swipe of frosting, he thought about how important it was for it to be just right. If the bottom layer was the foundation of everything, each layer of icing was the glue that would hold it together.

"Is this plate important?"

She leaned over and traced the tulip edge. "It was my mother's. All special occasions were served on this plate." She traced over the biggest chip. "This was my father's birthday." She moved to a smaller chip. "This was my high school graduation. Gage tried to take the last piece, and I grabbed the dish so hard it flew from our hands like a frisbee. It sailed through the open kitchen window and landed on a bush outside. The edge chipped, but the plate survived. This plate will outlive us all." She lifted the plate to show the signatures on the bottom. "For us, it's like a family bible. Everyone signs it. The plate might not be perfect and pristine, but it's seen my family grow up."

As she put on the second layer, he thought about her story.

"What a nice tradition." He had nothing so special as a plate that witnessed important events. He would have to think about building those kinds of memories with Avery.

One by one, they stacked the layers while he applied the sugary glue. When the five layers were stacked, he passed the spatula to Courtney.

"I fear I'm underqualified to do the good stuff."

She laughed. "Oh, you're not getting off that easy." She walked around the island and stood half behind and half beside him. She placed the spatula in his hand and placed her palm over his. "How about we do it together?"

He coated the cake perfectly with her guidance, swirling the frosting to create tiny ripples and waves. When he was finished, she grabbed the spatula and scooped up the remainder of the frosting.

"Open up," she said.

He did as she asked, and instead of placing the frosting in his mouth, she smeared it across his lips.

She moved quickly to get out of his reach, running down a hallway, but he was too quick and caught her before she got too far away.

She squealed when his hands reached for her hips, and he did the only thing he could think of to stop her from attracting the kids' attention. He spun her around and kissed her.

CHAPTER ELEVEN

What was happening? Courtney stiffened when his lips met hers. The kiss was an odd sensation but a welcome one. It had been over a decade since anyone had kissed her. Not true ... Jesse kissed her, and so did her mother, but those kisses were not this kiss.

This was a stumble-against-the-wall kiss that sent tingles from her toes to the one gray hair at the top of her head that she found that morning.

It was a hot, all-over kiss that reminded her how much passion was missing from her life.

His lips were full and warm ... scratch that ... they were hot and demanding. His tongue slipped out, and she offered him a taste.

A moan floated in the air. She was pretty sure it came from her, but she couldn't be positive with her head buzzing so loudly.

"Oh my God, I'm so sorry," he said.

One moment she was in lip-lock bliss, and the next, she was standing there, head tilted, eyes closed, lips puckered, and alone.

Richard backed up so far, he was against the hallway wall. His shoulder pressed into Jesse's second-grade T-ball picture.

Courtney reached forward to grab it so it wouldn't fall to the floor when he stepped away. Too late—he dodged her reach, and the picture crashed to the hardwood floor, breaking the frame and the glass.

"Oh hell, I'm so sorry."

Hurt and anger bubbled up inside her like a cauldron.

"Stop being sorry. That's the worst. I can take rejection, but don't ever be sorry for me."

He stopped and stared at her for a moment. "Sorry, for you? What the heck are you talking about? I'm sorry I didn't ask to kiss you first. I just ..." He shook his head. "I let my teenage boy take over. He saw a beautiful woman with a wicked sense of humor, and he jumped the gun."

He rubbed at his stubble—stubble that left a delicious burn on her face.

"You jumped the gun?"

He walked toward her and set his hands on her shoulders. "Yes. I'm a single father of a girl and try to pay attention to who I am as a man because everything I do teaches my daughter what she should expect from men. If a boy walked up to her like a caveman and kissed her, I'd be upset for her."

She let the bubbling cauldron fizzle to lukewarm.

"I'm not upset. I rather liked the spontaneity." She lowered her head, trying to hide the blush she knew was pinking her cheeks. "I loved the kiss. Do you know how long it's been since I've been kissed?"

He shook his head. "About three minutes, I'd say."

"Before that, it was eleven years, one month, fifteen days, and some hours." She made up the number because it was funny.

He smiled. "Could you be more specific?"

"I have no idea how long, but it was before I found out about Jesse. I think I was still using Lip Smacker's lip gloss."

"I always loved the strawberry."

She smiled. "Me too, but the grape runs a close second."

Two heads peeked around the corner.

"Did you throw that frame at my dad?" Avery asked.

Courtney looked at the broken wood and glass littering the floor.

"Why would I do that?"

She shrugged. "My mom used to."

Courtney turned to Richard. "Did she have good aim?"

He frowned initially but then smiled. "She never played T-ball."

"Jesse, get the broom and dustpan. Once this is cleaned up, we'll head out to dinner if that's okay with Mr. Shipton."

The kids took off down the hallway to the kitchen. "It's Richard, or because my behavior was appalling, you have permission this once to call me Dick." He looked toward where the kids had disappeared. "Besides. I think we've graduated past the level of where we need last names."

She moved sideways as soon as the kids rounded the corner. Richard's hands dropped from her shoulders.

"Ooh, according to Adelaide Phelps, we're probably on the second layer." She bent over and picked up Jesse's photo.

Richard took the broom and the dustpan from Jesse's hands and quickly cleaned up the mess.

Courtney liked that he didn't have a problem helping around the house. There were too many rules regarding gender, and while she liked a man to act like a man, she thought that those who were self-sufficient were sexier.

"We have several options for dinner. There's Atomic Pizza or Little Italy. We could also do Chinese. What do you want?"

Avery whispered in Jesse's ear, and Jesse whispered back.

"Little Italy, please. They have ravioli," Avery said.

Both kids looked up as if they could barter with their smiles even though the choice was theirs.

"Little Italy, it is. Let's go. I'm starving," Richard said.

After that kiss, she was famished as well, but it had nothing to do with food. She'd been attention-starved for years, and Richard just opened the floodgates to feelings and emotions she hadn't permitted herself to indulge in for years.

"Are we ready?" Richard asked.

Was she ready? Though she'd dressed up for dinner out, she'd done it because it was polite to look her best. That was what she told herself, but the truth was she was attracted to Richard. And up until a few minutes ago, she hadn't considered him someone she could or would pursue. He was like her boss, and everybody knew that a person shouldn't mix work and pleasure. But then he kissed her and muddled it all up.

"Yep, let me get my bag." She walked past him into the living room and grabbed her purse from the entry table. She would have to reevaluate everything. "Your car or mine?"

He opened the door so that everyone could exit. "I'll drive."

They climbed inside the Suburban and drove toward downtown Timberline. Through the pine trees, the setting sun cast an orange glow. If she didn't know better, it seemed the fire inside her had jumped into the forest and burned behind the trees. Her fire wasn't angry hot, but a low simmering heat that came with unquenched desire.

As they approached the restaurant, Richard pulled into the valet parking. To Courtney, it felt like a date-night thing to do. She had to remind herself this wasn't a date. This was a celebration for Avery getting her smile back and a thank you for all the meals she'd fed them.

Whatever was happening between them wasn't wise to pursue. She had to remind herself of all the reasons men were bad for her.

They interfered with logic.

They let her down.

They always left.

She probably could fill a notebook with other reasons, but those three were the most important.

The door opened, and a smiling young man dressed like he was boating in Venice said, "Welcome to Little Italy."

"Thank you."

He opened the door and helped Avery out.

She came immediately to Courtney and took her hand.

"You have a beautiful daughter," the young man said.

"Oh, she's..." Courtney looked down at Avery, who was showing off her new teeth. "She is beautiful." There was no point in explaining that Avery wasn't hers. He wouldn't remember them past the tip Richard pressed into the kid's hand. Jesse stood by Richard, and they walked side by side to the front door.

She glanced at their reflection and saw four people who could have been a family. They weren't too dissimilar in looks to throw out a DNA connection. Richard was dark-haired, and she was blonde. The kids fell somewhere in between: Avery, a dirty blonde, and Jesse, slightly lighter than that.

"Welcome," the cheerful-looking host said. "Family of four."

Jesse laughed. "We're not a—"

"Yes, four." Courtney didn't mind playing along. It was kind of fun pretending she was in a different situation than she truly was.

Not that being a single mom was bad. There were lots of perks. She never had to say, "wait until your father gets home," like her mother did when she was a kid. Her rules were king or queen in her case. What she decided was what she did. And with that, the consequences were hers too.

She stared down at Jesse with pride. He was an amazing kid. They say it takes a village to raise a kid, and she had one. It all started with supportive parents and a brother who was always there when boy things came up that she didn't feel entirely qualified to speak about.

The host led them into what he called Mama's Room, which was filled with pictures of Italian women cooking.

"Shall we start with calamari or antipasto salad?" Richard asked.

"Can we have both?" Jesse asked. "I've never been here; only to the grocery store they have next door."

Courtney sighed. "Honey, we are guests of Mr. Shipton's, and ordering too many things would be rude and wasteful."

Richard chuckled. "Not ordering both would be criminal."

She looked around the room at all the mamas staring down from the pictures and could almost hear them yelling, "Mangiare."

"It's too much, and he shouldn't have asked."

Richard smiled. "It's too much for one, but we're a ..." he smiled, "... family of four, and I bet we can wipe out both without much trouble." He reached over and ruffled Jesse's already messy curly top. "That was a good suggestion. Why have one when you can have both?"

"Daddy?" Avery looked at her father. "Can I take Jesse to the Pope room?"

"It's okay with me if it's okay with his mom."

Avery looked at her with eyes that Courtney couldn't refuse. "Go ahead, but you both behave."

Avery laughed. "Oh, don't worry. Everything in the room is glued down, so even if I got mad at him, I couldn't throw a thing."

Courtney wanted to laugh, but instead wiped her hand across

her brow. "Whew. I'd hate it if you two couldn't eat your food because you were missing your teeth."

They scampered off, leaving Courtney and Richard alone.

There was an awkward silence, and she filled it in with the first question that came to mind.

"Will you tell me about your wife?"

CHAPTER TWELVE

"You want to know about Cadence?"

The waiter came over and took their order for appetizers and drinks and then left.

She shook her head. "It's none of my business, but on occasion, Avery mentions her mother, and I don't know how you'd like me to handle that."

"What does she say?"

"Not much, but random bits about her mom dying in a car accident with another man and how Megan Fitzsimmons called her mom a whore." She made a fingernails-on-a-chalkboard face. "As I said, it's none of my business."

The waiter brought his iced tea and Courtney's Chianti, which he insisted she have when she ordered a glass of water. The kids got some Italian soda that no doubt had enough sugar to keep them pinging off the walls for hours.

It broke his heart that Avery had unanswered questions, but she wasn't old enough to know the truth. Even if she were, he wouldn't tell her. What good could come out of tarnishing the memories she had of her mother.

He took several sips of tea before he started.

"Cadence died in a car accident with her lover." It still pained him to say those words. "Michael Fitzsimmons was driving Cadence when they crashed."

Her hand immediately covered his.

"I'm so sorry."

"Me too. I'm sorry for lots of reasons, but mostly because I wasn't enough."

"Obviously, you loved her, and she broke your heart."

He looked down at where their hands met and turned his over to hold hers. It seemed as if Courtney could use comfort as well after hearing part of his story.

"Adelaide Phelps' cake is a good life lesson," he said. "You probably shouldn't ice the batter before you bake it."

Her head cocked left. "Obviously, you didn't follow the steps."

He shook his head. "Not a single one." He chuckled. "Well, maybe a little of the first layer. We were attracted to one another, or so I thought. I was attracted to her, and she was attracted to my job. At least the benefits she thought she could have being married to a pilot. But remember, I'm colorblind, so that limited my options. I'm a day flyer, and I pilot what most people call puddle jumpers—short flights from here to Denver or Vail and back. Occasionally I go to Colorado Springs, but that's not often. The timing is too close. If I take the flight, it's usually to fill in for someone who's sick, but the turnaround sometimes makes me do an overnight and that doesn't mix well with single parenting."

Courtney sipped her wine and nodded. "I bet that's incredibly tough to juggle. Thank you for sharing."

He wasn't much of a sharer of information, but then again, he didn't have anyone to share with. His parents were gone. He was an only child, and his friends disappeared when he became a single father. His history with Cadence weighed him down, but telling Courtney made him feel lighter.

"I've never told anyone. It's not something you open a conversation with. 'Hi, I'm Richard, and I wasn't enough for my wife, so she looked to another man to give her what she needed.'" He shrugged. "It's nice to be honest with someone. What about you? Do you want to tell me about Jesse's father?"

She laughed. "I already did. I blurted three words that sent him running. As far as I know, he's probably still sprinting. 'I am pregnant' can change a relationship."

He looked at the embossed tin ceiling. "They sure can. I was halfway finished filling out the divorce papers when Cadence said those words. We'd only been married for two years, but she had as many lovers. At first, I wasn't even sure Avery was mine, but when I saw her tiny little body, it didn't matter. I held my little girl and knew she couldn't be anyone else's."

"My father used to tell me that any man could be a father, but it took someone special to be a daddy," she said.

The waiter slid between them and set two plates of appetizers on the table and took their entrée order before he left. Richard ordered spaghetti and meatballs for himself and the ravioli for Avery. Courtney ordered a lasagna for her and Jesse to split.

"You don't have to conserve money. I can afford dinner."

She smiled and took her hand off his. It had been there for so long, he'd forgotten it, but the minute she pulled away, he felt the loss.

"Oh, it's not that at all. I know Jesse, and he'll gobble up the appetizers, and then he'll be full." She glanced sideways to the table on the left. "Besides, have you seen those serving sizes? That's enough to feed a family."

"Speaking of family." He watched from the corner of his eye as the two kids raced for the table and took their seats.

"Calamari," Avery said. "Yummy." She took a ring, dipped it in red sauce, and shoved it into her mouth.

"Avery," Richard said. "Table manners."

She let out a sigh but kept on chewing, her cheeks bulging with the too-big bite. Every once in a while, he'd see her wince, but he expected it as the dentist told him the flipper would take some getting used to and might cause sore spots the way any denture would.

"Aren't they octopus?" Jesse asked. He was a little more reserved in his attempt to taste. He picked up a fork and turned over several before piercing the smallest ring he could find.

"They're squid," Richard answered. "Which are like cousins to octopus but also snails. They come from a family of mollusks called Cephalopoda. Cephalo for head and poda for feet."

Both kids looked at each other and laughed.

Jesse dipped his ring into the marinara sauce and popped it into his mouth. He chewed it a few times and swallowed.

"It tastes like a rubber band."

"You eat many of those?" Richard asked.

"Oh, he's had a few." Courtney dished up salad plates for everyone. "Jesse grew up at the bakery. It used to be called Sweet Eats, but it only served bread. My father thought it was a great play on our name, but it was poor branding, and people were often disappointed when they came to find pumpernickel instead of pie. Anyway, Jesse spent a lot of time in the office with me, and he managed to find any rubber band within reach. I was so afraid one would get twisted around his intestines that I finally banned them from the business."

"That seemed like a wise and motherly thing to do."

She laughed. "It was financially driven. Each time he ate one, I rushed him in for X-rays. Those aren't cheap without insurance."

"You don't have insurance?"

She shook her head. "We can't afford it."

He might not be rich, but at least he had benefits.

"You need insurance. You saw Avery's bill at the dentist. Imagine what it would have been without it?"

"I'm working on it. Once Jesse is old enough to stay on his own after school, I'll get another job, one with benefits. Right now, I'm sticking with my guy."

The term "her guy" sounded nice. He wondered what it would feel like to truly be her guy. Not her son, but the man who came home to her each evening. He got a glimpse of that in the time she'd been watching Avery.

"You should let me pay you to watch Avery." He had tried, but she refused.

"We had a deal."

"No, you had a deal. I'm a smart man and said yes, but this arrangement wasn't supposed to last forever. You pick her up and care for her and help with homework and feed her. That's more than I expected, and I'm sure more than you bargained for."

"I'm enjoying my time with her. She's not a bother at all. She's an angel."

He almost choked on his pepperoncini. He pointed to his daughter. "We are talking about my Avery, right? She can be sweet, but it's generally when she wants something." He looked at the kids who were putting calamari rings on each finger but paid no attention to the adult conversation.

"She's a girl. She obviously learned very early how to play you."

He laughed. "I am a sucker for a pretty smile."

The waiter brought their main course, and as Courtney pointed out, the portions were enormous. Rather than eat one thing, they decided to eat family style and share. By the time the plates were empty, they were all stuffed.

"How about cannelloni for dessert?" the waiter asked.

"No," Avery said. "We have love cake at home." She snickered. "Jesse and I decorated it while you were kissing Ms. Courtney in the hallway."

He and Courtney stared at the kids with their mouths open. There was no use denying it; they'd been caught, and he didn't know what to do.

"You decorated the cake?" Courtney asked.

When he looked at her, a lovely blush pinked her cheeks, and she was more beautiful than before. Embarrassment looked stunning on her.

Jesse shrugged. "I watched while Avery used all the sprinkles." He rolled his eyes. "She put a big pink sprinkle heart in the center."

Avery narrowed her eyes. "It's a love cake, stupid." She turned to Courtney. "Why do boys have to be so dumb?"

There was a bang under the table, and Avery yelped. "Jesse kicked me."

Courtney smiled. "Crisis averted," she said, no doubt referring to the talk about the kiss.

"No kicking. What did we talk about the other day?" She used a mom voice that would send any kid into hiding.

"Never hit a girl." Jesse hung his head. "I didn't kick her. My shoe did. Besides, she called me names."

"Avery," Courtney said just as sternly. "You know how much name-calling can hurt. Just last week, you told me people were being mean because you lost your teeth."

Avery crossed her arms in a huff. "They called me grandma."

"You didn't like it, though, right?"

"No, because I'm not a grandma. I'm ten."

"Jesse isn't stupid or dumb either. Words are just as hurtful as that kick under the table. Sometimes, words are more painful

89

because you don't forget them, whereas you'll probably forget the kick in a day or so. Either way, you're both wrong and should apologize. Best friends don't mistreat each other, and if they do, they apologize quickly because losing your best friend is awful."

The kids looked at each other and then apologized, and everything was back to new.

He looked at Courtney and mouthed the words, "Thank you."

He paid the bill and walked out with Courtney and the kids. With each moment that passed, a consistent thought ran through his head. How had he survived without her?

As they drove back to her place, the car was silent.

"What are you thinking?" she asked.

He couldn't tell her he was thinking about their next kiss or how he'd love a real date. It didn't seem wise, but it seemed wonderful.

"Just wondering how you did that back there?"

She laughed. "I'm a master at manipulation too, I guess. You have to be when you have kids. If they don't like broccoli, you call them trees. If they don't like fish, you tell them it's soft chicken." She laughed. "For about four years, everything in our house was chicken. It was the only way he'd eat."

He glanced at her briefly before focusing on the street again.

"You're amazing."

"Not really, I'm just me."

He pulled into the driveway and stopped, and both kids unbuckled and raced to the door, yelling, "Cake."

When he was certain no one was watching, he turned to her.

"Can I kiss you again?"

She unbuckled and leaned forward.

"Yes, but do you think it's wise?"

CHAPTER THIRTEEN

"Wise?" Richard asked. "Probably not, but I'm throwing caution to the wind. My brain says it's a bad decision, but the rest of me is saying kiss the girl."

His lips pressed against hers. It wasn't a strip-off-your-clothes kind of kiss but a sensual slow burn that started on her lips, seamlessly moved into her brain, and then raced through her veins like heated syrup. It was hot and sweet, and she knew it wouldn't be enough, even if they stayed there and kissed all night.

As her lips opened and his tongue gently caressed hers, the porch light came on and they shifted to their sides of the car as if they were teenagers caught by spying parents. In this case, they were being summoned by the kids who wanted what Avery called love cake.

"I guess we should go. That layer of love cake won't last long if two kids are in charge."

Richard exited and rushed around to open her door. She loved that he was still in possession of a gentleman gene. In this day and age, it seemed like the world was in every-man-for-himself mode, but she was a woman who liked it when a man opened her door or pulled out her chair.

She was raised by a father who embraced old-fashioned values mixed with modern day common sense.

As they moved up the sidewalk, he rested his hand on the small of her back. If there was ever a day when she wished Gage was having a sleepover with her son, it was today.

A decade was a long time to go without intimacy, and the kisses she shared with Richard ignited a hunger in her that wouldn't be satisfied anytime soon.

"It's about time," Jesse said as they walked in the door.

"All good things come to those who wait." Courtney smiled because the icing on her son's lower lip told her he hadn't waited at all.

Avery pointed at Jesse. "He stole part of the heart."

When Courtney glanced at the cake, she saw the sprinkles were missing from the center of the pink heart and hoped it wasn't an omen of things to come.

"Who wants cake?"

The cacophony of "I do, I do" filled the air. Life was never boring or lonely with Jesse, but having Richard and Avery there made it feel complete.

"Jesse, get the plates, and Avery, you get the forks." She nodded to the knife block on the counter and looked back to Richard. "You get the knife."

As everyone did their part, Courtney stared at the *Recipes for Love* book and said a silent prayer of thanks to Adelaide Phelps whose recipe created a perfect moment in her life.

She cut small slices, and they took their plates to the table. Everyone seemed to have a chair that belonged to them and sat in what she considered their seats.

"How are the teeth?" Courtney asked.

Avery took a bite of cake and smiled, showing the rainbow of colors. As soon as she swallowed, she answered.

"They're good. A little sore here." She tipped her head back and touched her tongue to the roof of her mouth.

"I'm sure that will go away soon," her father said. "You just need to build up a kind of callous."

"Eww, that sounds disgusting."

Richard held up his hands and showed where the skin on his hands was tougher from where he held the yoke.

"I don't think you'll get a rough patch like this." He rubbed at the areas where his body had built reinforcements. "But your mouth will adjust."

She smiled again. "Or I could eat cake and ice cream all the time."

Jesse laughed. "Almost worth getting your teeth knocked out for."

Courtney frowned. "Don't get any ideas, son. If you knocked your teeth out, I'd feed you chicken broth and scrambled eggs."

"That's not fair. Why did Avery get ice cream?"

Richard held up his hand. "She also got soup."

"Chicken noodle," Avery said. "But I didn't eat the celery."

"You don't like celery?" Courtney asked.

"It was too hard so I couldn't chew it." She licked the frosting off the fork. "My mom used to make me ants on a log."

The table got silent for a second, but Courtney didn't want anyone feeling uncomfortable. Avery needed to talk about her mother. No matter what happened between Richard and Cadence, Avery was a child, and her memories were all she had left.

"Celery, peanut butter, and raisins?"

Avery nodded. "Sometimes, she'd use blueberries."

"Mom does that." Jesse added, "The ants can be anything from chocolate chips to nuts." He shrugged. "We use whatever we have. We're kind of poor so we don't waste."

Out of the mouths of babes.

"We aren't poor. Poor is when you don't know when your next meal is coming or where you're going to sleep at night. We are on a budget, but that's very different from being poor."

Jesse hung his head. "Fine, but it feels like we're poor most of the time. All my friends are getting new shoes for Little League this year, and I'm still in last year's shoes."

"Do they work?" Richard asked.

"Yes."

He smiled. "Do they fit?"

Jesse nodded. "Yes, but they're not the ones I wanted."

Richard set his fork down and leaned back in the chair. "I remember a year when I was playing football and all my friends got new cleats, but I didn't. By the end of the first week of practice, two of my friends were benched because the blisters on their feet hurt so bad they couldn't play. Newer isn't always better."

She had told her son that numerous times, but it never sunk in. Watching him listen to Richard was interesting because Jesse hung on each of Richard's words. She always knew he needed a male influence and her father and brother had served well in that capacity, but Gage was busy with the bakery and Chloe and her father was gone. It was obvious that he craved male attention.

"What about you, Avery? Would you like to play ball?" She probably should have asked Richard before she brought it up, but since she was the one watching the kids after school, and Avery would have to attend practices, it made sense to offer her the opportunity to join.

"Isn't that for boys?"

Courtney laughed. "Nope, it's gender neutral."

She looked at Jesse and then at her father. "Can I?"

Richard rubbed his jaw. "You want to play ball?"

"I'd rather take ballet, but I'm happy to try it."

Richard smiled, and it warmed Courtney's insides. He had the type of smile that was like sunshine. The minute the corners of his mouth rose, the world seemed brighter.

"I should have asked before I mentioned it, but practice started today, and I thought rather than have Avery sit and watch, she could participate, but if you'd rather she took some form of dance class, I can figure out how to work that in too."

Richard shook his head. "No, I think Little League is good."

Avery bounced in her seat. "Do I get new shoes?"

Richard shook his head. "Nope, you can use the ones you've got."

"But they're from last year," she whined.

Jesse rolled his eyes. "It must be contagious. They got it from kissing."

Courtney couldn't stop the gasp that escaped. They'd been caught again.

"Were you spying?"

"Are you going to marry my dad?" Avery asked.

Courtney and Richard sat in stunned silence.

"Umm, this isn't about marriage, honey." Her heart rate ticked up. "It's about ..." What did she say? She wasn't sure what it was about. She was fairly certain it was about loneliness.

"It's about time we helped with the dishes and got you home to take a bath." The chair legs scraped on the wooden floor as Richard pushed away from the table.

The kids groaned, but they cleared their plates.

"You've got enough time for a single game of checkers while I help Miss Sweet wash the dishes."

The kids bolted from the kitchen to the living room.

"I'm sorry about that. I'm pretty sure Avery thinks kisses create babies. By the time we get home, she'll have her new baby brother's or sister's name picked out."

"Might be time to have the birds and bees talk with her."

He groaned. "I don't even know where to begin."

She looked past him to the living room where the kids were fully focused on the game. "You might want to start with kissing. Then move on to the heavier stuff when she's ready for it."

"When she's ready for it? What about me? I'm not ready."

Courtney laughed. "Oh, you'll never be ready. As parents, we fake it until we make it. I'm just lucky that Gage had that talk with Jesse. I can't imagine how that would have turned out if I'd been in charge."

He rubbed his face with his palm. "Me either." He stepped to the sink and washed the dessert dishes. "Thank you for being there for us. I don't think I ever truly apologized for my rudeness. I wasn't having my best day when I met you."

"You think?"

"I know. I'd just left my doctor who informed me that my blood pressure was high, and I needed exercise. I found the early morning club hoping to discover some balance, but all I found was a group of women who were more interested in me than the walk."

"Oh, you poor baby. It must be terrible to be so attractive and desirable. That must really suck to have so many women attracted to you." The sarcasm dripped from her voice.

He set the last dish in the drying rack and picked up the hose from the sink faucet. Gripped in his hand, he turned and sprayed her directly in the face.

She stood there with water dripping from her chin. "Why did you do that?" In a quick move, she managed to get the hose from his hand and turn the nozzle toward him. A jet of cold water caught him in the face. They wrestled for dominance until the hose fell from her hand. As soon as the trigger was released, it stopped spraying, but the mess was already made.

"You're in so much trouble," Jesse said from the doorway

On a normal day, he'd be right, but maybe it was time to have a little fun. She'd spent so much time being a grown-up that she'd forgotten how to let her inner child out.

She pointed to Jesse and Avery who stood at the edge of the kitchen with their mouths agape.

"Come here, you two. You're just in time to help clean up."

While they were grumbling about the unfairness of it all, she picked up the hose, and as soon as they got close enough, she let them have it. She sprayed the two until Avery's hair hung in a sopping mess and Jesse's mop was stuck to his head.

By the time they stopped laughing, the kitchen floor was covered in water, but every face in the room was smiling.

"Can we do that again tomorrow?" Jesse asked.

"I don't think the floor could handle it," Courtney said.

They happily cleaned up together, and she walked them to the door. It was a bittersweet moment to say goodbye, but all good things had to come to an end.

Richard turned to Jesse. "Would you mind if I asked your mom on a real date?"

Jesse smiled. "You already kissed her ..." He held up two fingers. "Twice."

"I know, but since you're the man of the house, I wanted to make sure you were okay with that."

Jesse stood up taller. "Sure. I'm okay with that. Do Avery and I get to go?"

Richard shook his head. "Is it okay if I take your mom on the next date alone?"

CHAPTER FOURTEEN

Richard stood in front of the mirror and looked at the clothes he'd changed into. He always came to the same store and had the same clerk help him. It cut down on time when he didn't have to explain about his colorblindness. He had protanopia which made it nearly impossible to tell the difference between red, green, and blue. Everything seemed to come in shades of yellow and blue hues no matter what.

"What color is this?"

Dan, the clerk, smiled. "It's cherry red. You look good in red." Dan fixed the turned-up collar of the polo shirt, so it laid flat. "The pants are khaki, and if anything says 'I made an effort to look good for this date,' it should be khaki. It's kind of an un-color and everything goes with it but not everyone chooses it. As for the red, it's bold. It says 'look at me, I'm worth your time.'"

"Every color is kind of an un-color to me, including the red shirt." Growing up, he assumed everyone saw what he did, but the truth was they lived in high definition, and he lived in something that was slightly better than monochromatic.

"How'd you meet her?"

Richard chuckled. "It's a long story, but we had sort of a 'enemies to friends' kind of thing."

"The sex will be great then. That kind of passion can't be contained."

He hadn't thought about sex in a long time.

That wasn't true. He thought about it all the time, but he hadn't thought about expectations and relationships. He and Cadence jumped straight in, and that wasn't a good thing. He shook his head. The truth was the sex was really good, but that was all they were good at, and once that wasn't new anymore, they didn't have much left. They hadn't built the layers of love that were needed to sustain a relationship.

"I'm taking this one slow. Build a good foundation and you have a chance at building something stable and long lasting." He thought about the cake and the message. That Adelaide woman was wise.

He looked at himself in the mirror once more and nodded. "I'll take the outfit."

"It's a good choice."

Richard smiled. "I think I'm making some wise ones lately."

He changed back into his jeans and paid for his purchases. He had a few date details to take care of before he picked her up at six. He wanted to wash the Suburban and pick up flowers. He hadn't been on a date in years and wanted this one to be perfect.

As he left the store, his head turned to the right and his heart picked up its pace. Oblivious to his presence, Courtney entered the shop next to the one he exited. She was with another woman.

He knew he should have turned and walked away, but he was drawn to her like a moth to a flame, so he followed them. With large displays and full racks, he had no problem blending in and staying hidden.

"So, this is the first date?" the woman asked Courtney.

"We've been out but not alone." Courtney rummaged through a nearby rack. "I wore my nicest dress then and now I don't have a clue what to wear. Chloe, I need an intervention."

Richard wanted to laugh, but that would give up his super-secret hiding place behind the trio of mannequins.

"And you called me, which shows that you lack common sense. My idea of dressing up is putting on a clean chef's jacket and toque. I have no fashion sense."

"Maybe not, but you have good taste."

"How would you know? I'm always in uniform."

Courtney giggled, and his heart warmed. He loved the sound of her laughter. It was real and authentic and came from a place deep inside her. Her laughter was like striking gold, all rich and shiny and valuable.

"You chose my brother."

Chloe waved her hand in the air. "Oh, girl. Your brother was a pain in my bottom. I had to make a choice early on. I either needed to figure out a way to like him or go with my gut instinct and murder him."

Courtney pulled a dress from the rack and held it in front of her. "I feel the same about Richard. Most of the time I wanted to choke him, but there was something that drew me in."

"Probably the cologne. I think there's something to it. It's like a magic potion. Does he have nice cologne?"

Richard turned his head and sniffed. He wasn't sure if his cologne was nice or not; it was a habit. He'd been wearing it for years. It was just part of his morning ritual, like putting on his socks.

Courtney lifted her nose into the air. "I think you're right. Everywhere I go smells like him." She breathed in the air. "Even now I can smell it. He's like a freshly baked cinnamon roll."

He thought he was caught until Chloe smelled her shirt.

"That's me. I made the Danish this morning, but I'm telling you that cologne is pure sorcery. I can just nuzzle into Gage's neck and smell him all day."

Courtney put the dress on the rack and walked another rack over. "He kissed me."

Richard's ears perked up.

"Gage?" Chloe asked, and then made a gagging sound.

"Eww. No, that's just wrong. Richard kissed me." She made a sighing sound.

"Was it good?"

He managed to move when they moved but stayed hidden behind the merchandising. He was all ears for this part of the conversation.

"Toe curling."

"That good?" Chloe asked.

"I don't have much to compare it with, but it was good. Or maybe it's simply that I haven't been kissed in a decade."

Right then, he knew he had to up his kissing game so there was no question as to whether it was his kiss or her lack of them. He'd make sure that not only her toes curled but a shiver of desire raced up her spine.

"What do you think about this dress?" Courtney asked.

At this point, he was behind a shelving unit and couldn't see the women.

"What's the message you're trying to send? This one says, 'I'm ready for the first pew at the church.' That red one back there says 'I'll do you in the back seat.'"

"Oh my God. That is not the message I'm sending."

Chloe laughed.

It wasn't the laugh he loved. That belonged to Courtney.

Chloe's was kind of a ha-ha snort while Courtney's laugh was like music.

"What is the message?"

He leaned in closer to listen and knocked over part of the display. Knowing he'd be caught eavesdropping, he dashed in another direction, hoping to escape. Fate seemed on his side as he made it out the door without detection.

There was a pep to his step that he hadn't felt in a long time. He had a date with a beautiful woman that night.

He walked past Avery's favorite pizza place and thought about bringing the kids and the sitters dinner but wanted to check with Courtney first. He could have turned around and walked inside the store to ask but then there would be a lot of questions to answer, and he wasn't ready to fess up, so he called her.

"Hello."

"Hey, Court, I'm in the mall, and thought I'd pick up a pizza for the kids, your brother, and his fiancée for dinner. Are you okay with that?"

"You're in the mall?" Her voice squeaked at the last word.

"Yes." He wasn't a liar and didn't see a reason to tell her something different from the truth. "I bought a date outfit."

Her voice was muffled as if she'd covered the phone. He strained to hear what she was telling Chloe, but all he heard was a mumble.

"You bought a date outfit?" She sounded surprised.

"It's an important moment in my life, and I thought it deserved something new. You know, to celebrate the occasion. I'm wearing khaki and red."

"That's so sweet. I'm ... I'm at the mall too. Doing the same thing."

He smiled because, although he already knew, it was cute to hear her confession.

"You could wear a potato sack and look amazing." That was true. He never took note of what Courtney wore. Maybe he should have paid closer attention, but it wasn't important because it was what she wore on the inside that counted. He'd never looked at her after that first day and not seen perfection.

"Maybe I should save my money and visit the produce section of the grocery store instead."

There was a commotion on the other end, and he heard Chloe say, "Give me the phone." A second later, she said, "This is Chloe, and I'm the fashion coordinator. I'm also the babysitter tonight. Well ... Gage and I are co-sitting the kids. Did you say something about red?"

He chuckled because he wasn't the only eavesdropper. "I'm wearing a red shirt, or so I'm told. I have a bit of a colorblindness issue."

"Interesting. And where are you dining?"

He'd made reservations at the best restaurant he could find. "Mason and McHale's."

There was a moment of silence, and then he heard Chloe tell her she was getting the red dress.

"Hello," he said after endless seconds of silence.

There seemed to be another commotion.

"Sorry," Courtney said. "We were having a difference of opinion. Did you say Mason and McHale's?"

"Is it not good?" He'd never been there, but he'd heard great things about it.

"It's expensive."

He smiled. "You're not paying. Besides, you're worth it. You'll look great in a red dress. Get it." He knew tonight was a splurge for her, but he'd pay her back for the dress even if he had to "find" money on the floor and pretend she dropped it. Whatever she chose, Courtney would only make it look hotter.

"I'm bringing pizza. What kind should I get?"

Courtney asked Chloe and then said, "Anything is fine. No one is picky."

"They haven't met Avery."

"Avery is perfect."

He smiled as he walked toward the pizza place. "You're perfect, and I can't wait to kiss you again." He couldn't resist himself. "Do you think if I tried hard enough, I could curl your toes?"

She gasped, but he hung up. When his phone rang again, he was certain it was her, and he answered the call.

"Toe curling, that's a promise."

"Excuse me?" a voice that wasn't Courtney's asked.

He pulled the phone from his ear and saw it was the HR department.

"I'm sorry. Can I help you?"

"This is Daphne from HR, and I'm calling as a professional courtesy. I'll need to see you tomorrow in the office. The restructuring of the company has begun, and you've been reassigned."

"Reassigned?"

"Yes, but the choice is yours."

"What choice do I have?"

CHAPTER FIFTEEN

Courtney stood in front of the mirror, applying her final coat of mascara. Butterflies buzzed in her stomach from the excitement of having a date—a real date with Richard.

Next, she slicked on lip gloss and smiled. She found the strawberry Lip Smackers near the grocery store checkout stand when she stopped to get snacks for the kids.

She still couldn't believe Richard asked her that toe curling question. It was like he'd heard her entire conversation with Chloe, but that was impossible. Richard wasn't a man easily missed, and if he had been there, she was certain she would have known it.

"Mom." Jesse slid in his socks into the bathroom. "When are they coming?"

Excitement filled the air for everyone.

"Richard and Avery, or Uncle Gage and Chloe?"

"Both." He slid his socked feet back and forth on the hardwood floor.

She glanced at her nightstand clock and saw it was fifteen

minutes to six, and she wasn't even dressed. She pointed to the door.

"Out, so I can change. They'll be here any minute."

Jesse ran a few steps and then slid the rest of the way out the door.

"That boy will be the death of me," she said aloud.

The red dress hung from the hook on the back of the door. She let Chloe talk her into it, even though there would be no back seat anything going on. She had one back seat experience and that produced Jesse. While he was a blessing, she wasn't borrowing trouble. Besides, she had far too much respect for herself these days. She deserved wine and roses and a real bed when that time came.

As she undressed and slipped the soft fabric over her head, a thread of fear rippled through her. What if he was expecting that type of intimacy? Was she ready?

She shook her head and remembered their talk about the layers of a relationship and how he and Cadence had not built the foundation they needed to survive the shaky times. Surely, he wouldn't make that mistake twice.

As she dressed, her busy brain talked nonsense to her and told her this wasn't a lasting thing but a passing thing. She wasn't the kind of woman a man kept but the kind they tried out for a moment before they moved on to forever.

"Stinking thinking," she said as she slipped her heels on. "If you don't think you're worth it, how will anyone else see your value?"

That was a message her mother delivered on the regular when Courtney was feeling insecure and self-conscious. Love started with her. She was the mirror in which people would reflect their feelings.

She opened the closet door and stared at herself in the full-length mirror. The woman staring back was unfamiliar. She was not the college kid who let her libido run roughshod over her life. This woman was fierce in the red dress. She was worthy of love and anything else life had to offer, and she looked perfect for a night out at the finest restaurant in Aspen.

When the doorbell rang, Jesse yelled, "I got it."

She could almost see him skate across the wooden floor.

As she tuned into the voices, she heard her brother and Chloe. A few seconds later there was a squeal from an excited Avery and deep-toned greetings from Richard.

A soft knock sounded at her door, and she stood taller, getting her courage in check. Her heels click-clacked on the floor as she closed the distance between her and the rest of the evening.

When she opened it, there stood Chloe.

"You look amazing, and your date looks great, too. It's like you coordinated your outfits."

"You're a nut." She turned in a circle. "Is everything where it's supposed to be?"

"He's going to shatter some teeth when his jaw hits the floor."

"Oh, I hope not. Do you know how much a flipper costs these days?" She breezed past Chloe and walked into the living room to find Gage and Richard talking sports, but as soon as she appeared, the room went silent, and Richard's jaw did drop.

She was tempted to saunter over and close it for him, but she liked the way it felt to be appreciated.

"Stunning." He lifted the flowers he held in his hands and thrust them forward. "These are for you."

Avery bounced over. "Daddy picked them out himself. I wanted the pink roses dipped in glitter, but he said something about you being refinished."

"Refined," Richard corrected. "I said you were refined, and roses were perfect without the glitter."

She looked down at her dress. "I'd say I'm both refinished and refined, and I would have loved the flowers either way."

"Told you, Daddy. Glitter is always welcome."

He chuckled. "Unless you're in a cockpit, then it's questioned. I'm pretty sure my copilots think there's an after-hours show with dancers and glitter and feathers nightly once we park the plane." He looked at his watch. "We should go so we're not late." He turned to Chloe and Gage. "Thank you for watching the kids. Avery put the pizzas in the kitchen." His hand went to the small of her back. "Are you ready, beautiful?"

She nearly swooned.

"I'm ready." And she was. She was ready for whatever the night held.

He hugged Avery goodbye and walked Courtney out the door and to his car, which glistened like polished onyx. After he helped her inside, he rounded the car and took his place behind the steering wheel. Rather than start the engine, he turned toward her.

"You look amazing. That dress ... it's back seat worthy."

She gasped. "Oh my God, you were there."

He laughed and nodded. "I was, but I didn't want to interrupt."

She frowned and crossed her arms over her chest. "I don't know how I feel about you lurking and listening."

He reached over and took her hand. "I would have said something, but it was such a treat to watch your excitement about our date. I meant no harm."

She eyed him with suspicion and then smiled. "You better make my toes curl."

He smiled, but it didn't seem to hit his eyes, and that worried her.

They drove the twenty minutes to Luxe Resorts where the valet parked the car. The only time she'd been there was at the big reveal for The Great Bake Off. It was Luxe and out of her price range for everything, but she didn't feel like she didn't belong. Her mother raised her with class, and she could dress up or down with the best of them.

"Shipton for two," he said to the host as they walked into the restaurant.

Courtney glanced back at the lobby, which was decorated like a posh mountain lodge. A large table in the center of the room held dozens of small vases of fresh flowers that scented the air.

"Your table is ready, sir." The host led them to a quiet table in the corner and offered them menus. As soon as he left, their waiter arrived to take drink orders.

Richard ordered a pricey bottle of red wine. Next to arrive was the chef, who happened to be Chloe's sister, Gabby.

"I'm told we have VIP guests in our midst."

Richard cocked his head and then pointed to Courtney. "We have one. Isn't she lovely?"

Gabby nodded. "I'm Chloe's sister, Gabby, and I'll be preparing your meal tonight. Can I surprise you?"

Richard looked to Courtney for approval, and she nodded. As soon as Gabby left, she said, "I hope this dinner doesn't send you to debtors' prison. While I love being here, being anywhere with you would have been fine."

"You're a charmer," he said.

She giggled. "No one has ever accused me of that."

He reached for her hand just as the bottle of wine was delivered, but he ignored the waiter and stared into her eyes. As she looked at his, she noticed flecks of silver ringing his iris.

"Hard to believe how quickly life can change."

She picked up her glass. "Here's to being open-minded."

He clinked her glass. "Which neither of us were."

She shook her head. "Not true. If we were closed-minded, we would have never made it here."

He sipped his wine and caressed his thumb across the top of her hand. "You were kind and took Avery in and I appreciate it."

She thought about what he said. "I read a saying once that resonated with me. It goes something like this." She cleared her throat. "In a world where you can be anything, be kind." She glanced at him in his red shirt and navy sports coat. "You look really nice as well. Very dapper and put together." She took another sip of her wine. "I mostly see you in your uniform."

He touched his open collar. "I'm a little dressed down without a tie." He tugged at an imaginary one. "I hate them, but it's a part of the costume."

That was an odd way to describe his uniform.

"Do you like your job?"

He seemed to debate for a few seconds. "It's okay when it is and not when it's not. When I got my pilot's license, I wanted to open a flight school, but that wasn't in the cards."

"It's never too late."

"Sometimes you have to get real with yourself and admit when a ship has sailed. I'm a single parent who needs a stable income and insurance. What about you? What did you want to be when you grew up?"

She shrugged. "I'm not sure I had much choice. I always took care of the books at the business. It was assumed that I'd do that."

"But if you could do anything, what would you do?"

She grinned. "I wanted to be a princess once, but I didn't qualify."

The waiter delivered a beautiful charcuterie tray and disappeared once he introduced them to the items showcased.

"Royalty has qualifications?"

"Yes," she said with exasperation. "Can you believe there are certain birth requirements? And even if you're lucky enough to snag a prince, your family DNA has to come from a certain pedigree to be acceptable. I was certain William would choose me, but then he chose Kate." She sighed.

"William's loss."

She expected him to continue and say, "is my gain," but he didn't.

They enjoyed the charcuterie and the wine while discussing the kids.

"What does Jesse want to be?"

"Before you entered his life, he wanted to be an engineer and build stuff but now he says he wants to fly planes. What about Avery?"

"Oh, she's like you. She wants to be a princess, but she has a fallback plan."

Courtney smiled. "Something tells me if she set her mind on it, she'd succeed. Your daughter is tenacious."

"She has a strong spirit. That was a bonus she got from Cadence. I'm glad Avery is a force to be reckoned with. She has backbone and isn't afraid to try new things. I just want her to be true to herself and kind to others. I want her to have a moral compass, which was something her mother was lacking."

She could see the hurt in Richard's eyes and wondered if he still held a torch for his wife. It would be hard to develop a relationship with a man who pined for someone else.

"Are you still in love with Cadence?"

His eyes widened. "Lord no. At the end, we were a marriage of convenience. Only we were married, and it wasn't convenient for her. We stayed together for Avery. Which at the time seemed like the wise thing to do, but in hindsight, it only made everyone miserable." He hung his head. "I don't want to dwell on things, but I will say that we all do the best we can with what we have, and I didn't have enough for her. For that I feel bad because she needed more and in sneaking around to get more, she ended up dead."

Talk about a downer. Courtney regretted bringing up the former Mrs. Shipton, but she could now see that he wasn't pining for her, but rather punishing himself for her passing.

"We all make choices. She made hers. Having spent time with you, I'd say she made a poor one."

"Maybe I made a poor one the first time out." He frowned. "I'm trying to be smarter. My number one rule is do no harm. The last thing I want to do is disappoint another woman."

"I can't see you as a disappointment." She smiled and asked, "If you were to judge, where do you think we are if we were building a cake?"

CHAPTER SIXTEEN

Gabby arrived with the main course: a steak with grilled green beans, fennel and farro. He had no idea what fennel or farro was, but it smelled good and looked great. The distraction was nice, too, because he wasn't sure how to answer the question. He thought more about the cake at that moment than what was being served to them for the main course.

Usually, he wouldn't have reflected on that event much. They made a cake together. Many people baked, but there was something about that cake that made it special, and it wasn't the rainbow of colors. He didn't see that part anyway. It was the writer's words.

"I'll leave you then. Enjoy the meal. So that you know, I'll be whipping up something special for dessert." Gabby winked. "Unless you've got that already in the bag." She pivoted and walked away.

"This looks amazing. Have you ever had a top-rated chef cook a special dinner for you?" Courtney cut a bit of steak and put it in her mouth. The look on her face was pure bliss. "Oh my gosh, it melts in your mouth."

The look on her face was something he wanted to put there over and over again, but their lives just got complicated. Before the HR call, he saw a future with Courtney, but no future existed if they weren't in the same town. He knew what loneliness created. It created an opportunity for unhappiness, and in his mind, that was certain death.

Despite his gut twisting, he took a bite and had to agree that the meal was perfection. Everything was terrific, except the news from his company. He managed to coax more details from the HR rep. They were stopping the Aspen flights altogether. He had a choice to make. He could move to Cheyenne, Wyoming, or Denver, Colorado. Those were his choices if he wanted to remain employed. Taking one of those options was his only choice, which meant this dinner would be the last good thing he'd have in a long while.

He shook the sadness away and smiled. "I've had an amazing cook fix me dinner. She makes a mean pasta sauce. Everything she makes is Michelin Star worthy, including a Layer of Love Cake."

"Is that right?"

He held up three fingers. "Scouts honor." He leaned in as if to tell a secret. "I'd bet if she cooked this meal, it would be better too."

She laughed. "You have a lot of faith in that woman."

He sighed. "She's amazing."

A blush rose to her cheeks as her smile broadened.

"I'm just me." She swallowed hard. "But with you around, I feel like more."

"You don't need me to make you more. You're enough on your own."

She sighed. "Not true. I've never been enough, but I never give up."

"Tenacity is sexy." He was always attracted to strong women. The fascinating thing about Courtney was she didn't think she was strong, not if she didn't think she was enough, and how was he supposed to tell her that she would have been enough for him forever?

"Your expression turned serious for a moment. Are you okay?"

"I'm fine."

She lifted a perfectly-shaped brow.

"Is that a man fine or a woman's fine?"

He took another bite so he could formulate his thoughts and give her an answer that made sense. At this point, nothing was making sense.

After a long, drawn-out sigh, he said, "I'm not fine."

"Oh, Richard. What's wrong?" She set her fork down and reached for his hand. "Are you feeling okay?"

"You asked about our cake layer."

The blush deepened, and she shook her head before pulling her hand back. "It was a bold question, and you don't have to answer it."

He moved the fennel around the plate. It wasn't his favorite, but the farro was good.

After setting his fork down, he looked at her. He loved her blonde hair and the eyes he could swim in. They were the color of a spring sky. Looking at her was like laying in a field of flowers looking to heaven.

"I want to answer it. How silly is it that the words of a woman I've never met have resonated so deeply with me? Her advice is simple and basic. I think as humans, we muddy it all up and complicate things. I can only speak for myself, but I'm attracted to you, which is layer one."

"Layer one is good." She picked up her glass and took a sip of wine.

"That's the thing, we sailed past layer one and straight to layer two."

She laughed. "Oh, I wouldn't call it sailing past the layer. We had words, and two broken teeth, and an almost-call to social services. I'd say we hobbled to layer two, but yes, we got there."

He slid his plate aside. His stomach hurt because he had to tell her the truth, and that would hurt them both.

"I thought we were heading to layer three." He let his head drop. He wasn't sure if the weight he bore was too much or if he didn't want to see her face when he said the next part. "But we aren't."

She stared at him like she was waiting for the punch line.

"Is it the dress?" She scooted her chair back and looked down at what she wore. "Too bold, right?"

He shook his head. "No, it's stunning. You're stunning."

Her eyes seemed to cloud over as if someone poured milk in the midst. "Is it because I'm a single mother?"

He hated that a chuckle escaped, but it was a ridiculous question.

"I would have never been interested if you weren't single, and the mother part is amazing."

She picked up her glass and gulped the rest. "Not enough. I knew it going in, but there was a glimmer of hope that I'd be able to get to layer three of that damn cake."

He reached for her hands, but she pulled them away. She had every right to do that, but it felt like the nick of a razor against his skin.

"No, it's none of that. You are enough. It's just..."

"What? What is it?" She stomped her foot. "You promised me a toe-curling kiss." She threw her napkin on the table, picked up her purse, and turned to leave, but after a step, she stopped. "I could live with rejection, but you pulled me in and made me believe we had something special. Shame on you." She walked away.

He scrambled to pay the bill and chase after her. He didn't want her going home without an answer.

He rushed to the front of the hotel, half expecting to find her driving away in a cab, but there she sat, on the cement half-wall, waiting with silent tears streaming down her face.

He handed the valet the ticket and a tip and went to her.

"You walked out before I could explain."

"You don't have to, but I have one question for you."

He owed her whatever answer she needed. "Ask it."

"Why did you go through this whole charade if you had no interest in me."

The Suburban arrived, and he helped her inside before rounding the vehicle and taking his seat. He pulled away and drove slowly toward Happy Hollow.

"I'm interested. I would still give you that toe-curling kiss if you wanted it."

"I don't understand." She swiped at her cheek, and he deduced she was still crying even though he couldn't see her tears from where he was.

He pointed to his outfit. "I got a new date outfit because I was so excited. I had the flowers and spritzed on cologne. I'd talked myself in and out of a thousand things this night. Part of me wanted to take you to my home and make crazy passionate love to you, but I thought about the cake. We were building a solid foundation for something wonderful."

She made a choking sound, and he knew she was crying again. "'Were' is the keyword."

"Yes, but not because of you."

She jabbed out and slapped his arm. "You don't get to do the 'it's not you, it's me' thing. Don't you get it? It's always me. What man leaves his pregnant girlfriend?"

"An idiot. I would have never left you."

She yanked at the seatbelt so she could turn to face him. "Are you listening to yourself? You are leaving. Words like 'were' aren't forever kinds of words. They aren't stable like cement. They're quicksand words. Toppling the foundation of what we built."

He pulled off the road to the curb and killed the engine.

"Listen to me. It's not you. It is me. Well, not me exactly, but my job. I'm being transferred."

She stared at him in silence.

"You're really leaving me?"

CHAPTER SEVENTEEN

"It's not a choice I'd make if I had another choice, but I don't."

She crossed her arms over her chest and growled. "We all have choices, and I'm never anyone's. While that might sound selfish, just once, I'd like someone to choose me."

He reached out to touch her, but she melted into the door, trying to avoid his touch because there was no use feeling it when it was fleeting. By tomorrow, he'd be in her past with no hope of a future.

She tugged at the fitted dress, feeling so stupid for buying it. Maybe Chloe was right. It was a back seat dress, and that's all it was intended to be.

"Courtney, like me, you're a single parent. I know you understand the choices and sacrifices we make for our kids. If you want a new outfit and they need shoes, you get shoes. If you're tired and want to sleep but they need help with homework, you do homework. It's what we signed up for when we became parents."

He was right. Avery had to come first, but she was so tired of coming in second. She spent her life with the loveliest young man

—Jesse—and yet she was lonely. Anyone who says they can live without romantic love and intimacy hadn't lived in her skin. She craved affection the way she craved chocolate before her monthly cycle, and she hated to admit it.

When Jesse was younger, she didn't feel it as much, but she felt the loss as he grew up and needed her less. Maybe that was it. Perhaps it wasn't that she needed a man as much as she needed to feel valued.

"I understand." She hung her head in shame. She knew he was making the right decision. But his decision would change many lives. She'd grown to love Avery. Each time she picked the kids up from school, she had a purpose past being a mom to Jesse.

Avery needed her as much as she needed the sassy but sweet little girl. Each time she cooked dinner, it was with intention. Not that she ever fed Jesse mediocre meals, but feeding a family made it feel more significant than it probably was. Each meal she made gave her a chance to nourish them beyond food. She put a piece of herself into planning and felt proud when they loved what she offered.

Then there was the cake ... Adelaide Phelps' Layer of Love cake. When they baked it together, it was more than a cake. It was a commitment to try something new and scary. Trying her hand at love, but maybe that kind of love wasn't in her future.

"You're quiet," he said.

She shook her head. "There's not much left to say but thank you." She let her sigh slip out.

"What are you thanking me for?" He cocked his neck from side-to-side, making it pop.

"The moments. They were lovely."

He stared at her for a few seconds. "You truly are amazing. I just throw a curveball at you, and you're thanking me?"

A weak smile lifted the corners of her lips. "You gave me a

glimpse of what happiness can feel like. I may never have seen that without you. Yes, it's painful to watch it slip away, but I think I've always known that my life's path was different."

"You are worthy of love. You've just loved the wrong men."

"Were you the wrong man? Is that my problem? I'm attracted to the wrong kind of man?"

He flinched like she'd pricked him with a sharp knife a dozen times. "I'm the right man, but the timing is wrong."

She turned to face the front. "And that makes you the wrong man." A lump stuck in her throat. She would have loved to have seen where they would have ended up, but maybe it was good this way. She'd go home and pretend all was well for Jesse, and then she'd climb into bed and cry into her favorite pillow. "Can we go? I'd like to relieve my brother and Chloe of babysitting duty. They have to be at the bakery early."

"Right." He shifted and started the car, and they were on their way.

"I'd still like to give you that toe-curling kiss," he said.

Her heart rate sped to what felt like double time. She leaned against the glass to stop the dizziness. She craved that kiss too, but she would have to decline. It wasn't wise to tease her emotions. Another toe-curling kiss would tell her heart that anything was possible when she knew in her head it was not.

"I don't think that's wise. Let's stop while we're ahead."

He tapped the brakes, which jolted the car and made her turn to face him.

"Are we ahead?"

At least he was feeling something. She wasn't sure what it was. Was it sadness like her? Maybe it was regret that they'd started something in the first place? With men, it was hard to tell. They rarely wore their emotions on their sleeves. At least that was her experience.

"Listen, we both learned something from this. You never thought you could love again. And I'm not saying you loved me, but you have to admit that what we had together was special. Our families melded together perfectly, and that's a gift. All it proved was that it is possible to find something special with another."

"If I were going to love someone, you are the perfect recipient."

She hugged herself tighter, hoping direct pressure on her heart might stop the emotional hemorrhaging. She hated to admit it to herself, but she had fallen hard for Richard. If asked if she loved him, she wouldn't be able to lie. What she felt could only be love.

He pulled into the driveway, and while she waited for him to round the vehicle to open her door, she pulled up her figurative big girl pants and put a smile on her face.

When he opened the door and offered her a hand, she took it.

"When will you tell Avery?"

He took a deep breath and let it out slowly.

"Tonight, when we get home."

She nodded. "Okay," she squeaked. That lump in her throat grew impossibly large, and she had to swallow a few times to dislodge the emotions. "Let me know what I can do to help."

"You never even asked where I was moving."

She turned to face him and stared into his stormy blue eyes. "It doesn't matter. All I know is you're not going to be here."

He nodded and placed his hand at the small of her back to guide her up the walk to the door.

She pulled back her shoulders and put on her happy mom's face as she entered the house.

In the living room were her brother and Chloe, who were asleep on the couch, and Jesse and Avery sitting on a blanket in the middle of the living room eating popcorn and watching Disney's *Apple Dumpling Gang*.

Avery let out an, "Awww, it's not over yet. Can't we stay until it's finished?"

Courtney was hanging on to her emotions by a thread. "Sorry, kiddos, but it's time to go. We can pick up where you left off tomorrow." She walked by Jesse and ruffled his hair. "Go brush your teeth."

Gage and Chloe stirred.

"Date night finished already?" Chloe rubbed her eyes. "Everything okay?"

Nothing was okay, but there was no use dwelling on the negative.

"Sure, the kids have school." She tapped her brother's shoe because he had fallen back to sleep. "Get up and take your wife home." They weren't married, but the commitments were made. Rather than an engagement ring, Gage bought Chloe the stand mixer she always wanted and couldn't afford. That right there was love. "You can let yourself out. I'm going to change." She bent down and gave Avery a fierce hug. "I'll see you tomorrow." As she walked down the hallway, Richard called out to her, but she didn't turn because the tears were already running down her cheeks.

WHEN COURTNEY ARRIVED at the school, Jesse and Avery were waiting, but they weren't wearing their usual smiles.

"Hey, guys. I thought we'd go to the bakery for a treat. What do you say?"

Avery's head hung so low her chin touched her sternum.

"You knew last night, didn't you?"

Courtney had two choices. She could fess up or play dumb, and playing dumb wasn't in her lane. She had always prided herself on living an authentic life and didn't want to stop doing that now.

"I did."

Tears ran down Avery's cheeks. "Why didn't you tell me?"

Courtney led them to her beat-up SUV and got them buckled in. As soon as she took her seat, she turned to face them. "It wasn't my story to tell you. Your father had to explain the whys, hows, and whats."

"I'm not going." She crossed her arms and harumphed.

"I don't think you have a choice."

Avery frowned. "There's always a choice."

Rather than argue, Courtney started the Jeep and drove toward the bakery. Avery's statement sounded exactly like she had the night before. Yes, there were choices, but wise decisions were important.

"You have to trust that your father made the right choice for you both."

"It sucks," Jesse said. "I had it all planned out. You and Avery's dad would get married, and Avery and I would help take care of the new babies."

Courtney wanted to cry because somewhere deep in her heart, she had the same dream. Only Jesse and Avery wouldn't be the babysitters but loving siblings. It was a far-off dream, but it sat there waiting for fruition. Now it was like a seedling that would never get enough water to thrive and would wither and die.

"Oh, honey, we weren't anywhere close to that scenario."

"But you dated and kissed," Jesse said.

She nodded as she pulled into the spot in front of the bakery. "We did, but that's just the beginning. Love takes a long time to grow."

"Nuh-uh, I love you already," Avery said.

"I love you too, squirt, but it's different. You're easy to love."

"Daddy isn't loveable at all. It's his fault that all the good things leave our life."

Those were powerful words for a ten-year-old and completely untrue.

"Avery Shipton. You take that back." Courtney felt compelled to defend Richard. "Your father is making grown-up decisions that will provide you the kind of lifestyle you need to prosper in this world. If you think he made those decisions lightly, you're wrong. And as far as loveable ... your father is the most loveable man I've ever met." She opened the door and got out. Instead of waiting for the kids, she walked to the bakery door.

As Avery got out of the car, she heard her say, "I told you she loved him."

Poor Richard would have his hands full with that one. She was cute but cunning. Sweet and sassy. She was everything Courtney would want in a daughter.

As they entered the bakery, Chloe whispered into Gage's ear, and he nodded. She looked at the kids.

"Pick out a cookie while I talk to your ..." She shook her head. "Mom."

She grabbed Courtney's arm and tugged her toward the office. "Are you going to tell me what's happening?"

After they closed the door, Courtney moved the Kleenex box closer and took a few. She explained what had happened and sank into the seat behind the desk to cry.

"Tell me one thing, and be honest. Do you love him?"

CHAPTER EIGHTEEN

Richard walked into human resources and asked for Daphne. She was the woman who called and informed him of his transfer, so it made sense to talk to her.

He was led down a corridor to a small office where a frazzled woman with graying hair sat behind a desk half her size.

"Have a seat," she said with a sigh.

He slumped into the old seventies-style chair that looked like an upholstered box with wooden arms.

She pointed to a white plastic Mr. Coffee sitting on the file cabinet. "Help yourself." It had probably been around as long as the chair. It was half full of what looked like crude oil.

He had enough problems and some kind of dysentery before his flight home wouldn't be welcome.

"No thank you. I've just had a cup." He didn't want to offend but coffee from that pot was a hard no. "I'm Richard Shipton."

She looked up and pushed her glasses to the bridge of her nose.

"Did you decide?"

He shook his head.

"Are you sure there aren't other options?"

Her shoulders slumped. "You've got three: Denver. Cheyenne. Unemployment." She shuffled through the files on her desk. "Flights end in Aspen in two weeks so you have time but I'd like to pencil you into the schedule."

He'd given this a lot of thought since last night. He'd had a lot of downtime since he broke the news to Avery. She ran to her room and locked him out. This morning, she wouldn't even speak to him.

"What are the pros and cons?"

She frowned. "I'm not a life coach." She rubbed her chin. "Wyoming has lots of space. Denver is crowded. Choose what suits your personality."

He thought about Courtney and the conversation they had. He closed his eyes and saw the tears she'd shed because of him.

"What suits me is to stay in the Aspen area."

"Okay, so unemployment it is."

He held up his hand. "No, I have a daughter who likes to eat."

"Look," she said with a level of exasperation he'd only seen when Cadence didn't get what she wanted. "I'm not your therapist, your mommy, or your psychic. I can't tell you what to do. I just need an answer."

Feeling worn himself, he whispered. "Denver. I'll take Denver." Saying it out loud caused his gut to twist painfully.

"Done. I'll have you on the schedule in Denver in two weeks."

"But I need to find a house and move."

She held up her hands. "I'm not a real estate agent."

He rose from the chair. "I got it. What about time off to house hunt?" She turned to her computer. "Looks like you've got about forty-five days saved up. I'll put you on paid leave as of now."

"Let me get back to Aspen first."

She rolled her eyes. "I'm not a travel agent."

"I'll start paid leave tomorrow." There was no way he was giving up his shift and having to take a jump seat back home. "Thank you," he said as he turned.

"Glad I could be of help."

If his life wasn't so darned out of sorts, he would have laughed. Daphne was not what he'd call helpful. She was like going to a burger drive-in and finding out all they had left were ice, fries, and veggie bites when all he wanted was a burger.

WHEN HE PULLED up to Courtney's house, no one rushed out the door to greet him. There was no bear hug from his daughter or special handshake from Jesse.

The boy had become the son he never had. Over the weeks, he'd played catch, helped with homework, got his butt kicked in checkers, and got fleeced for money for after school ice creams. He loved every minute.

He trudged to the front door knowing Avery would probably give him the cold shoulder. She screamed at him last night and all her arguments were valid. She had friends. She was happy. She was doing well in school. She even tried to negotiate a new job for him saying he could work for Courtney, and they could live at her house.

He wasn't sure she understood the situation, and that Courtney wasn't in a position to hire him for anything. The poor woman didn't have insurance. All his arguments to defend his decision were too complex for her ten-year-old brain.

He knocked at the door and waited for someone to answer. That someone was Jesse.

"We're in the kitchen baking." He turned and walked away.

Richard went straight to the kitchen where Courtney smiled, but Avery's tiny little mouth stretched into a thin line. Anyone who bet on nurture versus nature hadn't met his daughter. She was so much like her mom in many ways from her appetites to her demeanor, but Avery's heart was bigger, and he knew eventually she'd come around.

"What are you making?" he asked.

"Same cake but with different layers," Courtney said.

He lifted his brow. "You can change the layers? I thought they all meant something special." His heart sank at the thought that the meaning of the cake could change. It was so special the way it was.

"No, Daddy," Avery said in a stern, "you're in trouble" voice. "We're not changing the love. We're changing the flavor."

"Oh." That made sense. "Can I help?"

Avery smiled for the first time since yesterday. "Only if you're a believer."

He took off his jacket and laid it over the stool. He loosened his tie and lifted it over his head. No use in having to retie it. He simply rolled it and placed it in his pocket.

"I'm a believer."

Avery grunted. "If that was true, you'd stay."

He sighed. There was no use responding. It would ruin the night because Avery would press and press and when she didn't get her way, she'd cry and then shut down.

"What do you want me to do."

Courtney pushed the book forward. "Why don't you reread Adelaide's story. It helps as we stack the layers." She pointed to the five cakes already baked.

He picked it up and started.

"The first layer of love is the beginning of everything. In this cake it's the first thing you'll put down. Some would call it attraction, but I'd call it flavor. For this cake, it's a rainbow of colors and flavors, but you may want to choose chocolate or spice. We like what we like."

Because he wasn't sure what flavors awaited, he asked.

"What's the flavor of the day?"

Jesse smiled. "It's chocolate. We are rotating layers between dark and milk. Three dark and two milk chocolate."

He nodded. "Is there a reason you all chose chocolate?"

Jesse answered again. "It's Mom's favorite when she's feeling down."

His gut twisted again. "I'm so sorry for everything."

She waved the spatula through the air. "We have to do what we have to do." Her smile was there but it was weak and didn't reach her eyes.

He lowered his head and continued.

"That second layer goes a little deeper; it's not the first hello, anymore. We're building something more, so we add on another layer which adds depth. For a relationship it might mean getting to know them better. There's nothing worse than being with someone who doesn't make you feel anything."

This verse tied his intestines into knots because for the last two years all he felt was anger and resignation, but Courtney changed that. She'd shown him there was a sun behind the dark clouds in his life. What if she was the only sun he could see?

He watched as Courtney stacked the layers and Avery spread the glue-like frosting.

"Layer three is the core. It's a big commitment to make a five-layer cake. As you stack the layers on top of each other, nothing will work if the foundation isn't solid. In love, this is where you find out the true ingredients of a person. What are their dreams and aspirations? Are they made from the same stuff you are? Remember that quality ingredients are important but mixing quality salt and quality sugar isn't going to taste as sweet. Compatibility is the key."

He and Courtney definitely had three strong layers. While they initially appeared to be opposites, they were actually an exact mirror of each other. She was alone and stayed alone for over a dozen years because she refused to let anyone in that could hurt her. He'd done the same after Cadence's death. How tragic that the first man she let into her life was him.

That brought on the thought of other men entering her life and he didn't like that one bit. He didn't want anyone else's lips to touch hers. He was positive that no other man would curl her toes from a kiss the way he would.

"We're waiting," Avery said.

He cleared his throat.

"One day my son Sam brought home a girl named Freya Gunther. She was a nice girl, but not "the" girl. I knew it because I could see that Freya was honey and my boy was sugar. One would think that sugar and honey would mix well since they're both sweet, but in my experience all that sweet will do is give you a bellyache and rotten teeth. One day Sam brought home Deborah. Now Deborah wasn't a pushover. That girl had some spice to her and mixed beautifully with Sam's sweetness. Too much of one thing is never good, so measure your ingredients wisely."

"What do you think we were?" he said out loud, even though it was meant to be a private thought.

"Perfect," she said as she placed the fourth layer.

He sat there stunned. Even though he'd hurt her, she looked at him like he hung the moon and a few stars as well.

"The fourth layer is when this cake gets serious. It's also the layer of love that requires a commitment. Once you stack it, there's no going back, so it's the promise layer. It's the almost there, layer. It's where you decide you're all in because no one makes a four-layer cake. This is where you carefully place more on the foundation you've built because if you've done it right there's no worry about it toppling over. If you've done it right, its staying in place."

He would have liked to have gotten to the fourth layer. He would have promised her the world, but the world had other plans.

"You are a fourth layer woman, Courtney."

She smiled and shook her head.

"I can hardly get past layer one. Everything seems to topple by layer three." She took a deep breath and let it out with a sigh. "Not everyone is meant to be in your life forever. We can wish they were, but the truth is, forever doesn't really exist. All we have is this very moment. So, we are here now, and now is my forever. Thanks for being here."

"I love being here. It's where I'd want to be forever if I had a choice."

She rolled her head from side to side.

"We all have choices, but sometimes we don't look outside the box. Fear of the unknown holds us back. I refuse to live in fear any longer. Thank you for coming into my life to show me that I, too, have choices. That sitting in my house and waiting for life to happen to me isn't what I'll choose from now on."

She placed the last layer on top and it didn't budge or topple or shift.

He wanted to ask her what her choices were, but he didn't. He didn't feel like he had a right.

"The fifth layer is where all the good stuff comes together. It's where you put the icing on and maybe some sprinkles and you celebrate the accomplishment because you've built the layers from the ground up. You've added the flavor that appeals to you and now you can enjoy its sweetness."

He wanted the damn five layers for himself.

"Anyway, the point of this recipe is to show that love, no

matter what kind of love, comes from the heart. Anything that comes from your heart is worth the effort. Put in the time and make sure to use quality ingredients and you can't go wrong. The important thing for both the cake and love is to build a strong foundation."

He closed the book and looked at the cake. Even with Avery's less-than-gentle spreading of the frosting, it was solid.

Once the cake was finished, Courtney cut thick slices. It hadn't occurred to him that the house didn't smell like dinner.

"Did you eat dinner?"

Courtney smiled. "Nope, we're having cake. Are you ready to live on the edge?"

CHAPTER NINETEEN

"Cake for dinner?" She'd had some bad parenting nights where they ate Lucky Charms for dinner ... several nights in a row, but this was not her status quo. She was a living, walking food pyramid. Every meal was nutritionally sound and contained the four basic food groups.

She attempted to justify.

"It won't kill them. Nor will it kill us to get in touch with our inner child. Besides, there's protein because of the eggs in the mix, and I'll pour glasses of milk. For dessert, we have a veggie tray and fruit tray." She gave him an I-can't-help-myself look.

"There you are. I thought some kind of body snatcher took over and the real Courtney was gone."

"Some habits are hard to break. Broccoli is in my blood." She picked up the plates of cake and moved to the table. "Is everyone going to stand there with their mouths hanging open or are we going to eat?" She hadn't told the kids they were doing a backwards day where they started at the end and worked to the beginning. "There's a saying that says, 'Life's short ... eat dessert first.'"

She hadn't had much sweetness in her life in the last day so this felt right. Not just for her but for the kids, too.

When everyone was seated, she held out her hands to say grace. She needed to remind herself that there were things to be thankful for despite the gloom in the air.

"Bless this cake and help it nourish our bodies and sweeten our dispositions. Amen."

After a round of amens, they all dug in. Jesse was right, chocolate was her go-to when things went to hell in a handbasket. When her father passed away, she lived on Hershey bars and chocolate milk for a week. She made sure to drink a chocolate protein shake three times a day and added super greens to it because a healthy body was a blessing and she couldn't afford to be sick.

"How was your day?" she asked Richard.

He took a bite and glanced around the table. Watching him was like watching a mouse trapped with a cat. He was the mouse.

"Oh, you know. Same old ... same old. I did a single flight to Denver and back. Normally, I would have picked up a Denver to Vail and back to Aspen flight, but I needed to talk to the woman at human resources." He looked at his daughter and frowned when she groaned.

"I'm not moving," Avery said.

"Avery," Richard said in an exhausted tone.

As she looked at him, his broad shoulders seemed to shrink in size.

"Well, I'm not. I'm staying here."

Richard looked at Courtney with pleading eyes.

She covered Avery's hand with her own. "Honey, sometimes grownups have to make tough decisions and they aren't always what we want, but in time you'll see it was best."

She shook her head. "I'm not moving."

Richard cleared his throat and opened his mouth, but closed it before saying anything.

"How about some veggies?"

The kids groaned, but nodded. They knew there would be a requisite number of bites they'd need to take to satisfy her mothering instincts.

She rose from the table and got the vegetable tray and the fruit tray from the refrigerator.

"Five of each and then you can watch thirty minutes of TV."

"Are you going to kiss my dad again?"

Courtney's heart sped like it was a mixer on high speed. The only thing she wanted to do was kiss him but was it wise?

The kids stared at her, waiting for a response.

She smiled.

"Maybe."

Richard's brow shot up. "Really?"

She laughed. "Weirder things have happened." After he left the night before, she regretted not kissing him. There were few things she had enjoyed in life more than Richard's kisses.

All day long she thought about them, and how it was one of the saddest things about him leaving. She had a mental list of all she would miss, and kisses was at the top.

He smiled. "I know. Who would have thought that Avery getting her teeth knocked out would be one of the best days of my life?"

"Hey," Avery said. "That was no fun."

Richard smiled. "You're right, but we all made it out alive. And whatever happens in the future, we'll figure it out too."

The kids ate their veggies and took their fruit into the living room.

"What did HR say?" she asked Richard.

"I have three choices. Cheyenne, Denver, or unemployment."

"Ouch." She gathered the empty plates and stacked them. "I know, right?"

"How much time do you have to choose?"

"None. I have to be in my new location in two weeks."

Her heart tumbled and she swore she heard a splat hit the floor. "What did you choose?"

Thin lipped and tight jawed, he answered. "Denver."

She remained silent as the reality set in.

"What about your house? Will you sell it?"

He nodded. "The agent arrives tomorrow. She says houses are selling at a premium so it might never make it to a live listing."

"Wow, I heard there were bidding wars. I hope you make a nice profit."

"It's paid for already so anything I make will go to the next purchase."

"Oh, wow." She knew the cost of real estate and he was sitting in a good position. "Will you buy right away in Denver?" Each word she said tore at her heart.

"I thought I'd take Avery with me in the next day or so to look at a few houses, but we'll have to rent in the interim. No place is going to turn around that quickly for us."

She considered his position. She, too, was a homeowner, but hers held a sizeable mortgage. The only person she knew who owned a house was her mother and that was because of her father's life insurance. Maybe that was how Richard paid off his home.

"Life insurance?" she asked, thinking he'd follow her train of thought, but the confused look on his face told her he hadn't. "You own your house outright which is amazing but you're also very young to have done that. I was asking if Cadence's life insurance paid it off?"

He laughed. "Are you kidding? She had a quarter of a million-dollar policy, but she borrowed against it to finance her fancy trips and spa days so when she passed there was about thirty-five left. I used ten to bury her and put the rest in a college fund for Avery."

"You're a very responsible man."

"When she died, I realized that I was all Avery had left and I needed to make sure she'd be cared for. I upped my policy to a million and I put every dime I had into paying the house off early. I figured if something happened to me, there would be enough to care for her."

Enough was all anyone needed.

He ate a carrot and stared at her. "I wish I had another choice."

She stared at his lips before she stood and took the plates to the sink.

"We always have choices." She turned and came back to the table and sat in his lap. She wasn't usually so bold, but she had a choice to make too. Did she wallow in sadness, or did she enjoy what she had in the moment? "You made yours." She brushed her lips against his. "Right now, I'm making mine."

"What choice is that?"

"To cash in on your promise of a toe-curling kiss. And maybe it will help you decide if the choice you made was right."

"There was no other choi—"

She silenced him with her lips. And as soon as the kiss began, the emotions of everything she felt for this man left her and she hoped entered him. She wanted him to feel her passion, feel her need, feel her heart. Mostly, she wanted him to feel her love.

Chloe asked her if she loved him and at the moment, she was too afraid to face her feelings, but the truth was right there in her kiss. She was in love with Richard.

The question was ... what would he do with that gift?

As their lips met and their tongues danced, she let her guard down and inhibitions go. She was always holding something back as if keeping it for herself would protect her, but not this kiss. This kiss was pure bliss. When he left, she wanted the taste of her lips to be on his and the memory of the kiss stamped in his brain.

As soon as her toes curled, she pulled away. He'd succeeded in his promise.

"What are you doing to me?" he asked.

She rose from his lap. "I'm loving you. Isn't it time someone did it properly?"

CHAPTER TWENTY

It had been three days since that kiss and it was all he could think of. He may have curled her toes but something about that kiss did him in. It was like her hope comingled with his dreams and created an alternate universe and he couldn't stop thinking about that world—a world where they were together always.

"I hate it, Daddy." Avery stomped her foot but the carpeted living room soaked up the sound.

"Honey, it's not permanent. This is a temporary place until we find a house." They'd driven to Denver to find an apartment. He thought having Avery help choose would ease the pain of moving but each place they looked at got the same reaction. It was too small, too many stairs, too ugly. There was always something wrong with it and he was getting worn.

"We have a house," she said.

He hadn't told her that it sold in the first showing.

"About that ... our house sold last night."

She stared at him as if his head had spun in circles and his eyes fell out.

"We might as well set up a box next to the dumpster outside like that other man. That's exactly what this feels like."

He rolled his eyes at her dramatics. "This is Highlands Ranch. No one is living in a box next to the dumpster and getting away with it." He looked at the agent for confirmation but she didn't give any. "Let's go."

As they left and rounded the corner to his Suburban, he saw a man living in a refrigerator box by the dumpster.

"I've got one more to show you," the rental agent said. "Follow me."

Avery gave him the silent treatment all the way to Cherry Creek.

"You heard the agent. This is the last one. You'll have to pick something because this is happening, Avery. There isn't a choice."

She crossed her arms. "There's always a choice. Maybe it's time you thought with your heart instead of your brain."

He knew she didn't come up with that phrase on her own. "Who told you that?"

She looked out the window and whispered, "Mom, the day she died."

He wanted to yell, "See what thinking with her heart got her," but none of that was Avery's fault. Her mother had chosen love above all else. She was willing to give up her home and family for it, and in the end, she died for it.

They pulled in front of a huge, gated complex and were waiting for the agent to press in the code.

"Look, Avery, there's a playground and a pool." As they wound around the buildings, he pointed out the benefits, trying to upsell it in her mind. It was one of the pricier units on the list, but it had all the bells and whistles. Surely, she would love it.

He parked next to the agent and turned off the SUV.

"Are you ready?"

She slowly turned to face him. "This one is fine, Daddy. I don't care anymore."

His heart sank with the sound of her defeat. "Of course, you do. Let's go see your room."

They walked side by side to Unit 3.

"It's the same as Ms. Courtney."

"Yes," he said. "Surely, it's a sign that this is the place for us."

She frowned before letting her chin fall so he couldn't see her face.

The agent spoke endlessly about the amenities while they walked through the apartment nearly as big as their house.

"The school bus picks up and drops off at the front gate at seven-thirty and three-thirty."

"What about daycare?"

She looked at Avery. "Isn't she a little too old to need a daycare center?"

He chuckled. "Though she's about thirty-five in the attitude department, she's only ten."

"I'm sure there's some teen in the complex looking for a few extra bucks."

He groaned because he was so done with the teen sitters.

Avery meandered around the two-story unit.

He watched her face for any sign of happiness but there wasn't one. She moved toward the door. "I'll be at the playground."

He had to believe that was a positive response despite her dead tone. "Okay, be safe."

"It's a gated community," the agent said.

"Crime has no address." It was true. Crime lived among everyone.

"Well, it doesn't live in Cherry Creek."

He didn't have time to argue. It was getting late and he needed to get on the road. "Will you send me the contract for this unit?"

She smiled. "Absolutely. Or we can head to the business center and fill it out right now." She was gung-ho to get him under contract. "All I need is a security deposit."

"I'll look over the contract tonight and transfer the money in the morning."

He could see her demeanor deflate like a popped balloon. "Okay then, I'll get it sent over right away. Safe travels back." She moved around the unit shutting off lights while he walked out to the playground where Avery sat on a swing that barely moved. Her eyes cast down toward the gravel.

"Hey little bird, how goes it? You want to hit that burger place you like on the way out of town?"

She slid from the swing and moved sloth-like toward the car. "I'm not hungry."

"Okay." He thought about the things that might lift her spirit and the only thing that came to mind was Jesse and Courtney. "What if I call Court and Jess and see if we can stop by. I'm sure there's leftover cake."

"Really, Daddy? Can we?" Her smile was brighter than a hundred-watt bulb.

"I'll call."

He did, and Courtney said to come on over.

They made the drive in record time. He didn't know why it felt like time rushed forward but that seemed to be the way of things. The good stuff always sped forward while the boring stuff seemed to stop time.

They had no sooner pulled into the driveway when the door flew open and Jesse ran out.

"Mom cut two big pieces for us and I have the checker game set up."

Avery lit up and took off toward the door like she was shot

from a pistol. The kids disappeared and Courtney showed up wearing worn jeans, a T-shirt, and a smile.

"Come on in. I saved you a piece too." She waved him toward the door. "Have you eaten yet? I've got some leftover meatloaf and mashed potatoes."

His stomach grumbled so loud, he was certain she heard it.

Even her laugh indicated that she had.

"Let's get you fed. You can't live off cake alone."

She fed him while the kids talked animatedly about their lives. Their biggest burden was who would win at checkers and who got the most frosting. He wished life was that easy but it wasn't. There were complications at every turn.

"Will I have Avery tomorrow after school?"

"I don't want to be a burden, but that would be great. I have contracts to sign and a moving company to hire."

Though she smiled, he could see the sadness in her eyes. Normally a clear vibrant aquamarine, they were now a milky blue.

"You're not a burden."

"I'm sorry things didn't work out better."

She seemed to sink into the counter. "They worked out fine. When I met you, I was positive I'd never feel love or longing or passion again. Knowing that you have to leave, I could go back to my old life and live it just fine, but you taught me that I'm worth more and that I am worthy of love. That first night we came back, I had a come-to-Jesus moment with myself. I hated that I was hurting. I hated that I allowed you to work your way into my heart. I hated you."

"Ouch." He pushed his plate away for a moment.

"Then I realized that had I not met you, I wouldn't have felt all those good moments too. Life is a balance of positive and negative. The thing is, if we don't know hurt, we can't experience joy. Thank you for showing me what it felt like to be wanted. I think that's what I've been searching for my whole life and now I know it's possible."

He moved the cake plate toward him. "Will you date someone else?" Just asking those five words pricked at his heart.

"I'm not looking for someone else." She stared right into his eyes. "It's hard to find perfection twice."

She grabbed her slice of cake and sat beside him. "I think good old Adelaide knew something about baking."

He took a bite and let the flavors hit every tastebud. "She seems to know a lot about love, too."

"That she does."

They ate their cake and watched Avery win the game of checkers.

"Time to go, kiddo."

After the requisite groan and complaints, they headed home. This time there was no kiss to keep him feeling warm inside.

Avery went straight to her room, and he decided to fill out the contract in the morning.

He fell asleep to a single question running on repeat through his head: was it better to think with his heart or his head?

CHAPTER TWENTY-ONE

"Brush your teeth," she called to Jesse. "We're leaving in twenty minutes."

She rushed around grabbing his lunch and jacket because she was certain if she didn't hand them to him directly, he'd forget. "Don't forget your homework."

"It's in my backpack."

She rounded the island and put his lunch in his backpack. She always doubled the treat because he shared with Avery. She didn't have the heart to tell her father that she didn't love the fruit snacks he put in hers.

The trill of her phone broke the silence and she picked up the call.

"Good morning, Richard," she said in a pleasant tone. His calls were her favorites. While he didn't normally call in the morning, it was a nice surprise.

"Is she there?" His voice was tight and clipped.

"Is who here?" The only "she" they had in common was Avery, but why would she be here?

"Avery. She ran away."

Courtney stumbled back as if she'd been punched in the chest. "Are you sure?"

Richard exhaled loudly. "I've searched the house high and low and she's not here."

"Did you call the police? Maybe she's been abducted." Jesse walked out with a look of confusion on his face. Hearing only one side of a conversation was confusing.

She covered the phone with her hand.

"Avery is missing."

Jesse's face turned white. "Did she run away?"

Courtney thought it odd that he deduced that from their limited conversation.

She spoke to Richard. "Hold on a second, okay?" Without waiting for an answer, she turned her attention back to Jesse. "Do you know anything about this?"

"No, mom." He shook his head, but she wasn't all that certain he was telling the truth.

"I mean it, Jesse. If you know anything, I need to know, now."

He slipped on his backpack. "I swear. I don't know anything."

"Then why would you assume she ran away?"

"Because she said she was going to."

Courtney threw her arms in the air. "Why didn't you say something?"

"Because I didn't believe her."

She obviously had more lessons for her son. When a girl like Avery said she was going to do something, it was pretty much a given.

"Avery ran away," she told Richard.

"I know, she left me a note."

Courtney growled. "Why didn't you tell me that in the first place?"

"I would have if given time, but you dropped me to talk to Jesse."

"Let's go, Jesse." She moved him to the door.

"Can you help me look for her?" Richard asked.

"Yes, let me drop Jesse off at school and tell me where to meet you."

He released a sigh of relief. "Can you come to the house? I don't think she's gone far so I want to start here and work my way out."

"I'll be there soon. Call the police, too. They can be on the lookout as well."

He was silent. "Do you think that's necessary? I think she's acting out of anger."

"Better to have lots of eyes looking out for her."

"I suppose you're right."

She hung up and rushed Jesse to school.

"Mom?" he asked from the back seat. He was old enough to sit in front, but she still felt he was safer back there.

"What, honey?"

"Can I come with you to help find her?" Concern filtered through his voice. He was genuinely worried.

"I think it's better if you stay in school. If she shows up there, you'll be there to support her."

He groaned and let out a big "dang" accompanied by a snap of his fingers.

At the school drop off, she gave Jesse a long and strong hug. It never occurred to her that he could be there one day and gone the next.

As she drove toward the address Richard texted, she worried for him because Avery was all he had left. She couldn't imagine the worry he felt but knew it had to be overwhelming.

She pulled in front of the big house with a sold sign out front.

She was barely out of the car when he ran out the door and wrapped her in a desperate hug.

"Thank you for coming."

She leaned back to take in his worried expression.

"Of course I'd come. I love Avery. She's like a daughter to me. The one I'll probably never get the chance to have." Having Avery around was a blessing and yesterday, when she wasn't with them in the house after school, it felt like a giant crater had opened up and sucked out part of Courtney's life.

He took her hand and led her up the brick sidewalk into the big gray stucco-covered house. It was so modern compared to her cabin-like home. They walked into a large entry flanked by a circular staircase leading to a second-floor landing. The entry floor was white marble, all hard and cold.

"Would you like some coffee?"

She wondered if it was wise to waste time having coffee when they could be out looking.

"Should we get going?"

"The police are on their way." He pointed to the kitchen island, twice the size of hers. On top was an array of pictures.

Seeing Avery's smiling face warmed Courtney but it was followed by an icy chill because those pictures were there because the police needed something to identify her from.

"Right. I'm glad you called them." She watched as his hands shook trying to get a K-cup into the machine. "You sit down, and I'll get that."

She moved him to the end stool and proceeded to make them both a cup of coffee. When it was finished, she took the seat beside him.

"I know she was unhappy. You should have seen her face at the last place we looked at. She looked like one of those puppies they show you on TV. You know, the ones at the pound who look forlorn and abandoned." He scrubbed his palm over his face. "I figured she would adjust to the new place, but I'm not so sure anymore."

"We all have to do things we don't like at times." She sipped her coffee. "Right now, none of that matters. All that counts is we find our girl."

"Our girl," he repeated and covered her hand with his.

It felt right. Over the weeks, Avery had become a large part of her life. If she were honest with herself, she was in love with them both. That was the thing about dating a man with a child. It was a double whammy to the heart.

The doorbell rang and Richard went to answer the door while she glanced around the large kitchen. His house was enormous, but it lacked warmth. Everything was hard and edgy, from the white stone counter to the sharp nickel handles. The black shiny floor would have been a nightmare to keep clean and to keep Jesse from using it as his personal skating rink. The kitchen opened into a vast living room with modern furniture. It was a high-end IKEA playground. As the voices grew closer, she took a last glance at the space around her. An entire wall was covered with pictures of Avery. One of them was with her mom. Like a moth to a flame, Courtney rose and walked toward it.

Her mother was stunning and everything Courtney was not, which made her wonder why Richard liked her in the first place. Maybe it was why he found it so easy to leave her. She wasn't his type.

When the two officers and Richard appeared, she moved back to the kitchen. It wasn't a long visit. They gathered the photos, the information, and took a photo of Avery's note which simply said: "I'm not moving. Sorry, Daddy."

As soon as the officers were gone, Richard sank against the island. "What if I can't find her?"

A lump rose to her throat, but she swallowed. This was not the time to break down. She needed to be strong for Richard.

"She'll be okay. She's smart and knows how to take care of herself. You've taught her well." She wasn't sure if that was the truth, but it sounded good, and she needed to boost his spirits, which seemed to be falling fast.

"What if someone abducts her?"

A shiver raced down her spine. "We can't borrow trouble. All we can do is look for her. We will find her." She gulped her coffee and put her cup in the sink. "Let's go. I'll drive."

She didn't wait for him to answer; she knew he'd follow if she led.

Like he did for her, she opened his door and waited until he was settled and buckled in before she shut it. On her way around the car, she said a silent prayer that they would find Avery right away.

Sitting in the driver's seat, she turned to him. "Where's her favorite spot?"

He smiled. "Your house."

"Okay then, we'll start there."

She took the quickest route to her house, but they found nothing, so they backtracked until they'd searched for her everywhere from the cemetery to the diner. Avery was nowhere. As the hours passed, Courtney's confidence at finding Avery started to dwindle. Lots could happen to a pretty little girl on her own.

When it came time to pick up Jesse, she was at an all-time low, but she plastered a smile on her face for Richard's and Jesse's benefit.

"Did you find her?" Jesse asked as he slipped into the back seat.

She shook her head in silence.

"Do you know where she could have gone?" Richard asked. "Has she spoken of any place she'd like to visit?"

He shrugged. "Disneyland, but I doubt she would have run away there. It's too far."

"I'm scared," Richard admitted.

Courtney took one hand off the wheel and reached for him.

"We'll find her. We won't stop until we do." She drove toward home, figuring they needed a bite to eat and another cup of coffee if they were going to continue.

As she pulled into her driveway, she smiled.

Curled up next to her carved welcome bear was Avery. She was sound asleep.

Richard leaped from the car before it was stopped and ran to his daughter, sweeping her into his arms and kissing her face like he hadn't seen her in a thousand years.

"Give them a minute, okay?" Courtney knew Richard needed time alone with Avery to talk over the situation. "We're going to walk past them and go straight into the house."

"But Mom, I want to say hi."

"I know, baby, but this is an important moment for them. How about you and I go inside and cook something. I'm sure Avery is starving, and I know Richard hasn't eaten."

"Can we make grilled cheese and tomato soup?"

That was always Jesse's comfort food which only proved he needed comforting as well.

"I think that's an excellent idea."

As they moved past, Courtney let her hand slide across Richard's back. "We'll be inside when you're ready." She glanced at Avery's tear-stained face. "I'm glad you're home, honey." That felt right, too. This was a home where Avery could be herself and feel like she belonged.

"Jesse and I will make something to eat."

They worked side-by-side with Jesse cooking the soup while she made the sandwiches.

"I wish they lived here, Mom. Our house is small but there's enough room for everyone. We could turn the playroom into a room for Avery and I can share my room with Richard."

She chuckled. "I'm sure he'd appreciate that. Will you give him the lower bunk or make him crawl to the top?"

Jesse frowned. "The top bunk is mine."

"Good choice."

"Can we invite them to live here?"

"That doesn't really solve their problem, sweetheart. Richard's job is going away."

She heard the door open and looked up to see Avery and Richard walking inside hand-in-hand.

"You guys hungry?" Courtney asked.

Avery broke free and ran toward her, throwing herself into Courtney's arms. Tears sprang from the little one's eyes.

"I'm sorry."

"Hey," she said, wiping the tears from her cheeks. "It's going to be okay."

"No, I don't think so. I love you and your stupid son."

Jesse grinned despite being called stupid. It was almost like he considered it a compliment.

"We love you too."

"Eww, yuck. I don't love her. I like her a lot. I mean, she's okay for a girl. If I could have a sister, she wouldn't be awful."

That was about as close to *I love you* as they were going to get from Jesse.

Courtney cradled the little girl in her arms, holding her and rocking her until she was sure the last tear was gone.

"You hungry?" she asked.

Avery nodded. "I walked here and all I had was an old cookie in my pocket."

Courtney ruffled her hair. "Best cookie ever, I bet."

She was shocked that she'd walked all that way. It was over five miles and the poor thing had to be tuckered out.

"Go wash up and I'll set the table." She put Avery down and the two kids took off toward the bathroom.

"You okay, Dad?" She looked at Richard, who stood leaning against the counter looking worn and weary.

He nodded. "I'm so relieved."

"Did you call the police?"

"Yes, right before we came inside."

She moved toward him and took his hand, guiding him to the table before he collapsed from exhaustion.

"You sit, and I'll nourish you."

He cupped her face. "You do that without the food."

She laughed. "Oh, you need more than me." She pointed to the steaming soup and the perfectly browned cheese sandwiches. "Let's feed you and we'll see how you feel after."

They sat down to eat like a family. Gone were Avery's tears and in their place was a smile. The whole meal, Richard stared at his daughter like she might disappear any second. The truth was, she could.

This was a great lesson in life. We have only the minute we're in. The past is behind us, the future isn't here, and the only minute that counts is the one we are experiencing.

For Courtney, the minute was perfect.

"Can you spend the night?" Jesse asked.

Both Courtney and Richard's eyes grew wide.

Richard looked at Avery's hopeful expression and turned to face her as if he was asking permission as well.

"Do you want to spend the night?" She'd never had a sleepover as an adult. She wasn't sure how that would work out. There were two youngsters in the house so there would be no funny business going on in her room no matter how desperately she wanted to experience Richard.

"It would be nice for Avery to be somewhere she feels happy."

Courtney knew he didn't want to wake up and find her gone again.

"Sure, Avery can sleep in my room, and you can have the bottom bunk in Jesse's room."

"Aww, Mom. Can't Avery sleep there just for tonight, and Richard can take the couch? It unfolds into a bed."

She couldn't help but smile. The two kids were smiling and nodding and a part of her wanted this family-like moment to last a little longer. She turned to look at Richard to get his input.

"I can do that," he said.

She thought about it for a minute and saw no reason to say no.

"It looks like we're having a sleepover."

CHAPTER TWENTY-TWO

The kids scampered off to play in Jesse's room, leaving him with Courtney.

"Thank you for helping today." He picked up the kids' plates and walked them into the kitchen.

"You would have done the same."

He nodded. "I would have. All you would have had to do is call, and I would have been there beside you." He rinsed the plates and put them in the dishwasher. It was the least he could do since he'd eaten up her day and her food.

"I know you would. You and I ..." She shook her head and waved him off.

"Finish what you were going to say." He wanted to hear her thoughts.

"It doesn't matter." She brought her plate over and stood beside him while he rinsed it and put it next to the others.

"It does to me. Tell me."

"I was going to say that we've built a good foundation and our friendship is solid." She turned around and leaned on the counter.

"That first day I met you ... you were cocky and arrogant and dismissive, and I couldn't wait to get you out of my life."

"And now?" He swallowed hard. He wasn't proud of the way he'd acted that day. He acted on autopilot. He was hardened by years of disappointment. It was all he knew and then she popped into his life to change everything he thought he knew.

"Now I can't imagine my life without you." She pushed off the counter and moved toward the living room, but he couldn't let her get away.

He pulled her back and tugged her into his arms. She didn't fight him; she melted into him. The way her body molded to his made him want so much more, but what did he have to offer her?

He tilted her head up and looked in her eyes.

"Can I kiss you?"

"You better." She lifted on tiptoes, reaching for him.

The kiss was soft and sensual. It was a dance where they swayed together tasting and experiencing each nuance. She tasted like Lip Smackers, and he couldn't get enough. Every sound she made, he ate up with his desperation to have more.

One thing he knew for certain: he'd never been kissed or had kissed anyone like this before, not even Cadence. It was like the ice around his heart had fully melted and the frozen organ thawed and started to beat again. The emotions were so overwhelming he was afraid he might cry.

Instead, he kissed her with more heart and passion than he knew existed. It was a kiss that said, *you are my forever*. The logical side of his brain reminded him that he couldn't keep her. The emotional side warred within him, screaming, *why not?*

With one hand at the small of her back and one placed between her shoulder blades, he held her tightly, wanting the moment to last.

"They're kissing again," Avery said from a distance.

Less than an hour ago he was searching high and low for his daughter, but in that second, he wanted her to disappear just so he could continue kissing Courtney.

The kiss broke, leaving both of them breathless. He could only speak for himself, but he wanted more of that.

"I should grab an Uber home and pick up a few things that we need. I can be back in a few hours."

Courtney seemed dazed but shook her head and smiled.

"Take my Jeep. It isn't fancy, but it works." She walked to the entry table and picked up the keys, holding them in the air and jingling them. "I'll make sure the kids do their homework and we'll have a late dinner. How about takeout Chinese?"

He smiled. "Perfect. I'll pick it up on my way back."

The two kids stood in the hallway and stared at them as if waiting to see if they'd kiss again and he wasn't going to disappoint. It wouldn't be a passionate kiss, but he wasn't missing an opportunity to touch those lips again.

As he walked by, he pressed his mouth to hers. "How did I get so lucky to have met you?"

She laughed. "Your shoe was untied."

He remembered her snarky response on that day.

"Yes, and you owe me a lesson in double knotting."

He took the keys and walked outside to her Jeep. It was old, but she took care of it. That was the thing with Courtney; she took care of everything around her, including him and Avery.

As he drove toward his house, he felt light in a way he hadn't in years. Maybe it was because the heavy weight of finding Avery was gone.

His path took him past the municipal airport. As he looked at the runway, he watched the biplane lift off. Behind it was an advertisement. He stared at the words: "Always choose love." Part of him knew that was the slogan for the jewelry store in town but part of him wondered if the universe was giving him a message.

He licked his lips all the way home just to get a taste of her. How was he supposed to give her up? As he pulled into his driveway, he looked at the sold sign. Everything was in motion. He had a plan, but was it the right plan?

CHAPTER TWENTY-THREE

What did a grown woman do to prepare for a sleepover?

The kids would be fine. All they needed was dinner, a snack, and a movie. But what did she have to offer Richard?

The first answer was clean sheets and a soft pillow. She rushed around making sure everything he'd need for the night was set.

While the kids did their homework, she pulled out the sofa bed and made it so it would be ready when he was. She even spritzed the pillows with her favorite lavender linen spray.

After she finished that, she set the table for dinner and whipped up a batch of cookies. She was tempted to try another recipe in the book, but she was a rule follower, and the rules were clear. One recipe and pass the book on.

She brewed a cup of tea and sat at the island reading through the Layer of Love cake recipe, marveling at how perfect it had been for her life.

The book never promised her love. It promised that she'd learn about love. The one thing she gained from the whole experience was that nothing would last if it wasn't built on a solid foundation.

As she considered her relationship with Jesse's dad, that was the problem all along. They had no foundation. All they had was a mediocre back seat moment.

All these years, she blamed herself and her lack of beauty, sex appeal, and whatever else that proved she wasn't worthy of love. Even that morning she'd looked at that picture of Cadence and felt less than, but she wasn't.

She didn't have to be part of the problem. A strong foundation began with two strong people, and she never gave herself enough credit. She was more than enough.

The book taught her that anyone who didn't see that about her was lacking.

She turned to the back of the book where an envelope was tucked into a pocket. She pulled it out and set it on the counter. While this was her book, it had been a joint effort, and she imagined it was only right that they read the last owner's note together.

A light knock at the front door drew her attention and she went to answer it. Standing there with flowers in one hand and a bag of Chinese takeout in the other was Richard.

"These are for you." He handed her the flowers. It was a mixed bouquet that she swore contained every flower that grew on the planet. "Beautiful."

"Yes, you are." He breezed past her to the kitchen where he dropped off the food and went back to her Jeep to get a bag that she assumed carried their clothes. "Are you hungry?"

She couldn't decide. She was hungry, but not for food. He'd kissed her like he owned her, and she was happy to be his. Sadly, the reality was that while her heart belonged to him, it was temporary. She had to remind herself that nothing had truly changed.

"I could eat." It had only been a few hours since they'd eaten soup and sandwiches, but strong emotions were as effective as exercise. Wasn't the brain like a muscle? If so, hers had been bench pressing heavy weights since the morning. "I've set the table. All we need to do is gather the kids."

"I'll get them." He walked to Jesse's room. "It's time to eat."

She put the white boxes on the table and opened several. "Did you buy the whole restaurant?"

He moved into the kitchen and washed his hands in the sink. "I wasn't sure what to get, so I got a variety."

"Are you planning on staying all week?"

He turned and smiled.

"Wouldn't that be nice."

She moved around him to get extra napkins. "It would, but I know it's not possible." Once the kids were seated at the table, she and Richard took their seats. She picked up the envelope from the back of the book and held it into the air. "It would appear that we have a task to complete."

They passed the boxes around and everyone chose what they wanted. She had beef with broccoli and shrimp with lobster sauce over rice. The kids went for everything that was deep fried and had sweet sauce like orange chicken and egg rolls.

"What's that?" Jesse asked.

She went on to explain that part of the agreement in making the recipe was that you got a note from the last baker, and you had to leave a note to the next baker.

"What does it say?" Avery asked.

"I don't know; let's open it and find out." She passed the envelope to Richard. "Do you want to do the honors?"

He took the envelope and ran his finger under the flap before pulling out a trifold paper. He opened it and smiled.

"I swear the universe is messing with me." He turned the page around and read out loud what he'd already memorized. "Never give up on a chance to fall in love."

"Eww," Jesse and Avery said together.

Richard reached over and mussed up Jesse's hair. "Wait until you're older. Some girl is going to make your head spin." He let out a whistle. "And when that happens, you'll think differently about love."

Jesse's expression turned serious. "Does my mom make your head spin?"

Normally, Courtney would have chastised her son for being so bold, but she wanted to know too.

Richard looked at each person, starting with Jesse, then moving to Avery, and ending with her.

"Your mom definitely makes my head spin."

"Then we can't move, Daddy. Don't you see ... we have to follow the rules. You always say it's important to follow rules."

He lifted a brow. "Obviously, I didn't enforce them enough. Don't talk to me about rules when you can't follow them." He didn't sound angry, just matter of fact.

"You can ground me for life if you promise to follow the rules too," Avery said.

"What rules, honey?"

"Adelaide Phelps gave us rules. Build a cake, you get love."

He shook his head. "That's not what she said. She said that building love is like building a cake. You need to do it layer by layer."

Avery let out a frustrated growl. "I know, and all the work we've done here will be wasted if we leave." She crossed her arms and let out a huff.

"Love is never wasted, Avery." Courtney passed out fortune cookies to each of them. "I believe that every person enters your life for a reason or a purpose. Not everyone is supposed to be there forever."

"Not true. Daddy and I are forever people."

Courtney couldn't argue with that. "You'll forever be important in my life."

Jesse held up his fortune cookie. "Talking about rules. You need to open the cookie and take out the fortune, but you can't read it until the cookie is eaten otherwise the fortune won't come true."

"But I don't like fortune cookies," Avery said.

Jesse shrugged. "Then I guess you don't get your fortune." He tore into the wrapper and cracked open his cookie, setting the fortune aside while he gobbled the cookie. When he finished, he picked up the tiny piece of paper and read it out loud.

"A stranger is a friend you have not spoken to yet." Jesse frowned. "I wanted it to say I'd win a million dollars."

Avery choked down her cookie and opened her fortune. A big smile spread across her face. "A dream you have will come true."

"What dream?" Jesse asked.

She buttoned her lip and tossed away the imaginary key. "I'm not saying, or it won't come true." She looked at Courtney. "It's your turn."

So she didn't get in trouble with Jesse, who was taking the fortune cookie rule seriously, she unwrapped her cookie, removed the fortune, and ate the cardboard-tasting cookie before she picked the paper up. She stared at it. "All good things come to those who wait," she said. She pushed Richard's fortune cookie toward him. "Your turn."

He held it up. "All the answers to my problems are in this cookie. I just feel it." He made a silly face and tore into the wrapper. He devoured the cookie and looked at the fortune. "Wow." He shook his head. "I think the universe is playing her hand in my life right now." He turned the fortune so they could see. "If you have something good in your life, don't let it go!"

Avery stood and pushed in her chair. "I rest my case."

"And there you have it," Richard said. "I swear we have a lawyer in our midst."

The kids cleaned the table while Richard stroked the fortune between his fingers. "So many weird coincidences today. I swear the world is telling me to stay."

She smiled at him.

"Would that be such a bad thing?"

CHAPTER TWENTY-FOUR

"No, but I would need a new plan and a job. I'm a pilot, and that's the only airline that serves this community. Staying is not a choice."

"We always have choices. Some are harder than others. My suggestion to you is to align your dreams with your needs. There has to be a middle ground. Rather than jump at the first opportunity, why don't you sit back and take it all in. When is the last time you took time for yourself?"

She had a point. He'd been on this endless roller coaster since he married Cadence. All ups and downs, without a straightaway to catch his breath. Then, after her death, he'd been treading water just to keep his head above it.

"Not that you've asked my advice but I'm giving it to you anyway. You and I have something special but let's take that out of the equation. It's just you and Avery and your job. You say you don't have choices and yet you're making a lot of them. Stop and take a break for a moment and take you and Avery into consideration. Right now, you're thinking about your job."

He shook his head. "That's not true. I'm thinking about Avery and providing her a lifestyle."

She stared at him expressionless for a moment. "Are you listening to yourself? What is a lifestyle if you hate your life? Can you honestly say you love what you do or who you work for?"

He leaned back in the chair. "I love my job but not the company."

"And yet, you're willing to uproot everything you have for them. Align your dreams and needs. The way I see it is you have some time and resources. You sold your house which gives you the money to make the best decision for you and Avery." She lifted from the chair. "I'm going to make some decaf coffee. Would you like some?"

He shook his head. "No, but do you mind if I leave her here for a few minutes while I take a walk to clear my head?"

Courtney placed the K-cup into the machine and pressed start.

"I think that's a good idea."

He walked to her and kissed her gently on the lips.

"I appreciate you."

She laughed. "Mwah? I'm your outer subconscious knocking on your brain telling you to pay attention. Sometimes the best decisions aren't the easiest."

He gave her another quick kiss and walked out the front door.

The smell of pine filled the air. He tipped his head back and let the sun warm his face. He'd spent most of his life above the clouds. Up there, the world was pretty clear. He had a job and a daughter and plugged along every day. But he never took the time to pay attention to what was happening around him until Courtney. He went from point A to B and saw nothing in between. But today he smelled the trees and damp ground and felt the cool air rush against his cheeks. The birds chirped as if saying hello. A squirrel scampered up a tree. The gravel under his feet crunched as he made his way down the street.

Small cabin-like structures dotted the landscape as he turned on Hocus Pocus Lane. He laughed because there was something magical about the neighborhood. Everything about Courtney bewitched him.

She made lots of good points. He let his job define who he was and where he went. He went over the conversation with Daphne, the woman from human resources. Not once did she say, "I'll help you with this." Her answers were short and to the point and mostly started with "I'm not." As he walked, he stood taller and picked up his pace. She made it clear when she said, "I'm not a life coach. I'm not your therapist. I'm not a real estate agent. I'm not a travel agent." She wasn't invested in his life. She had her own, and his didn't matter to her but the quality of it mattered to him. He replayed the rental agent's words in his head. "I'm sure there's some teen in the complex looking for a few extra bucks." He didn't want to go that route anymore. Up until last night Avery was good. She was happy—happier than he'd seen her in years.

Was he willing to sacrifice his happiness and hers for an employer who didn't see him as a real person? He was a job filler to them. He'd even bet that if he walked into Daphne's office tomorrow, she'd recognize his face but wouldn't know anything about him because she wasn't invested in his happiness.

"Align your dreams with your needs," Courtney said.

His phone rang and he looked at the screen to see it was Sara, the rental agent.

"Hello, this is Richard."

She let out an exhale. "I didn't get the contract."

Their conversation was typical of what he had with many people. There were no niceties. No hellos or how are yous. He was a means to her ends.

"Hello Sara, I hope your day is going well."

"Oh, yes, hi," she said.

He wondered if she realized how rude she'd been to simply blurt out his misstep.

"I apologize about the contract. I've had a family crisis but it's under control."

"Right, okay. Will you be sending it soon? This unit isn't going to last long."

Scare tactics were always a go-to but they wouldn't work for him today.

"If you need to rent the unit to someone else, that's okay with me."

She was silent for several seconds. "You're not taking it?"

He hadn't truly decided until that second. "No, I'm not. It turns out that the only people who want me in Denver are the ones that have something to gain. But what they don't realize is I have everything to lose if I go."

He was pretty sure she didn't know what to say, so instead, she hung up. He turned onto Magical Way and was filled with a sense of ease he hadn't known. His life was in total turmoil. In a week he'd be homeless and as soon as he got back to Courtney's he'd be jobless, but he was content. Finally for the first time in a long time, he was at peace.

He rounded the corner again to Courtney's street and found an agent placing a for-sale sign two doors down from Courtney's house. He looked to the sky to say thank you to the universe.

"I'll take it," he said to the woman.

She looked around as if he wasn't speaking to her. "The house? But you don't know how much it is."

"How much is it?"

She told him and he smiled. It was two hundred thousand less than he'd sold his for. "I'll take it."

"But you haven't seen it."

"I don't care. It's perfect. You see ..." He looked toward Courtney's house. "I'm in love with the woman two doors down. We are building a five-layer cake, and this is part of the process. I'm dreaming and aligning."

The woman stared at him like he'd grown an extra head.

"You really want this house?"

He nodded. "I do." He knew he should look at it but ultimately it didn't matter what it had because everything he needed was fifty feet away. "Draw up the contract." He gave her his number and walked back to Courtney's. At the door he knocked and waited.

Courtney opened it and smiled. "How did it go?"

"Best walk ever."

"I'm glad. What now?"

He pulled her in for a passionate kiss and when he released her, she stumbled back.

"Maybe you should take a walk again. I like what happens when you come back."

"If you liked that then you're going to love this." He walked to the living room. "Kids, I have an announcement."

They looked up from the television.

"I need everyone's undivided attention if you don't mind."

Jesse turned off the show and they sat staring at him.

He reached behind him to take Courtney's hand and he led her to the sofa and asked her to sit.

He pulled out his phone and dialed human resources, putting it on speaker and raising his finger to his lips to tell them to be silent.

"This is Daphne, how can I help you?"

"Hi Daphne, this is Richard Shipton."

There was silence and then shuffling of papers. "Oh, yes. What can I do for you?"

He knew she had to pull his file to remember who he was and that only reinforced his decision.

"I'll be sending my notice today." He looked at the kids and Courtney. "I can't leave my family for a job I don't love. I had to make a choice and I chose them and me."

"You're quitting your job?" Daphne asked.

"Yes, immediately." He hung up.

There was collective gasp from the room.

"We're not moving?" Avery asked.

He smiled. "We are, but we'll be close." He pointed over his shoulder. "I am buying the house two doors down."

"You what?" Courtney rose and rushed out of the room to the door, peeking outside to see the for-sale sign.

"That house?"

"Too close?"

She threw herself into his arms. "No, not close enough. You could have stayed here."

He laughed. "While I'm sure the sofa will be comfy, it's not my long-term plan."

She leaned her head on his chest. "What's the long-term plan?"

He hugged her tightly. "I'm building a strong foundation. Because what we have is special. We have all these layers, you and me, and I want them to last." He knew she got what he meant when she nodded.

"What layer are we at now?"

He smiled. "Oh, we're at the commitment layer. I just quit my job and bought a house because I'm in love with you and I can't imagine my life without you. Just wait until I make love to you."

She let out a squeak. "When will that happen?" She sounded almost breathless.

"I was hoping you didn't have any plans for the afternoon tomorrow."

She looked up at him with hope in her eyes.

"Are you inviting me to a sexy time date?"

"I'm inviting you into my heart." He smiled. "I mean, you already live there but I want you to unpack and make yourself at home."

"I think I love you," she said.

He kissed her and pulled away. "I know I love you. If you're unsure about how you feel, I promise by the time we pick our kids up from school tomorrow, you won't have any doubt." He would show her his love in a way that she'd feel to her core.

The kids finally showed up at the door and looked at the house two doors down. "That house is bigger than ours," Jesse said.

Avery smiled. "It has to be if we're ever getting a little brother or sister."

"Brother," Jesse said.

"Boys are stupid," Avery blurted. "That's why she needs to be a girl."

Jesse stuck his tongue out. "If she's a she then she is a girl."

They walked back into the house arguing all the way.

"Are you ready for that?" Courtney asked.

"Another baby?"

She laughed. "No, two kids arguing all the time."

"I can't wait. What about kids? Do you want more?"

She buried her head into his chest. "We can't disappoint them. They want a sister."

He laughed. "Jesse wants a brother."

She lifted on tiptoes. "Maybe we can give them one of each."

CHAPTER TWENTY-FIVE

Courtney woke to the smell of fresh brewed coffee and something sweet like pancakes. She stretched and yawned, slid out of bed, and into her slippers. After taking her robe from the hook behind the door, she shuffled to the bathroom.

If she could just get there without being seen, she'd be happy. She was certain her hair was all over the place and there was more mascara under her eyes than on her lashes. She hadn't followed her normal nightly routine of washing and moisturizing. Instead, she sat on the couch after the kids went to bed and kissed Richard all night, like a teenager whose parents were gone.

When they both couldn't keep their eyes open, she slunk back to her room, wishing he could join her, but he was right, she didn't want to confuse the kids or set a bad example.

She closed the door and flipped on the switch and smiled when she looked at herself. She was happy and it showed in her smile and her eyes. Her lips were swollen, but with passion.

"Women pay thousands to get lips like these," she said as she slid her fingers across them. "I got them simply by kissing Richard." She quickly brushed her teeth, washed her face, and managed to get her hair acceptable looking.

As she walked down the hallway, she heard the kids giggle, and when she turned the corner, her heart swelled. This was perfection.

Standing in front of the stove with her ruffled apron wrapped around his waist was Richard. The kids sat at the island with glasses of milk and smiles.

"Wow, can I hire you for the morning shift?"

He spun around and looked at her. A smile that lifted his lips went straight to his eyes.

"Would you like coffee?"

She nodded and took a seat at the end of the island. No one had ever really waited on her. She'd been the chief caretaker since Jesse was born. She certainly had never had a man besides her father prepare a meal.

The Keurig sputtered to its conclusion, and he mixed in the perfect amount of cream and sugar before handing her the mug.

"How did you know?" she asked

He grinned. "I paid attention. And I confirmed with the local expert." He nodded toward Jesse whose smile had doubled in size since she sat down.

"Daddy makes the best pancakes," Avery said with pride.

Richard held up the box of pancake mix that just needed water. "It's hard to mess this up."

Courtney laughed. "Oh, I've seen it done. Add too much water and you've got crepes and too little and they're hockey pucks."

He flipped the last cake and placed it on a platter, then set them in the center of the island.

"Eat up kids, your ride leaves in thirty minutes." Richard

pulled a stool next to Courtney and sat. "Hope you don't mind that I stepped in."

"Not at all. This is the best surprise ever. Poor Jesse gets a bowl of cereal or a breakfast bar. Pancakes are for weekends. You're spoiling us."

She took two pancakes and put them on the plate she'd been given. After a pat of butter and a drizzle of syrup she took a big bite. They may have been from a mix, but she was certain they tasted so much better because they were made with love.

She sat there and ate her two plus another, enjoying every bite.

"You look beautiful in the morning," Richard whispered.

"Are you sure you should be flying? I think you're sight impaired."

He kissed her cheek. "I can assure you that my vision is perfect outside the color thing."

"Pinch me so I know this is real."

He sipped his coffee looking over the mug. "It's about to get really real. You still up for our date?"

Her heart skipped a beat. Her body was screaming yes but her brain was giving her reasons in rapid succession as to why it wasn't a great idea.

He must have seen the panic in her eyes.

"We can go as fast or slow as you want."

She knew he'd never force her, but it wasn't that she wasn't ready. She was. It was the old voices coming back telling her she didn't deserve him.

He tapped her head gently. "Don't think with this. I can see it in your eyes. You're telling yourself a million reasons why you're not enough, but you are. You're exactly what I've been dreaming about."

How could a girl say no to that?

Once the kids were finished, he had them brush their teeth and get their backpacks and told them to wait for him outside.

He leaned over and kissed her slowly and sensually.

"I'll be back, and I can't wait to build this next layer with you. It's going to need a lot of icing and some extra baking time." He nipped her lower lip and she nearly fell off the chair.

"Hurry," she said, wondering where that sex siren breathlessness came from.

As soon as he shut the door, she bolted to the shower. She knew the morning would be life altering and refused to enter her new beginning with hairy legs.

In her estimation, she had about thirty to forty minutes to primp and spent extra time in her closet picking out her outfit. It made her giggle because she knew what she put on wouldn't stay on long. Her best guess was that the first time would be quick because they both needed to feel something, but the second time they would take a more leisurely approach.

She chose the sundress she'd worn that first night they had dinner. It seemed like a good choice for a beginning. She dried her hair and put on her makeup and walked into the living room just as Richard entered the house.

He stopped in the doorway.

"Wow. You didn't have to change. When I look at you all I see is beauty."

"Oh, yeah. Those plaid flannel pajamas were sexy."

He shut the door and stalked toward her.

"You could wear a trash bag and it would look good." He bent down and swept her into his arms. "Are you ready to start the beginning of the rest of our lives?"

He was already walking to her room. No answer was needed.

At the edge of the bed, he set her on her feet.

"I love you, Courtney. Never have those words felt so good to say."

Her knees nearly buckled, but he kept her steady.

"I love you too." She bit her lip. "I'd be lying if I said I wasn't nervous."

He chuckled. "I'd be lying if I said I wasn't nervous too." He sat on the bed and pulled her into his lap. "This is new for both of us, but I can assure you, there is nothing about you that I won't love."

She turned to straddle his lap and kissed him.

"I'm glad we're nervous together. It makes me feel more comfortable knowing this matters as much to you as it does to me."

"This is the beginning of everything. I want it to be special."

She giggled. "Well, if we muck it up, there's plenty of time for a do-over. The kids don't need to be picked up until three."

"I like the way you think."

She pushed against his shoulders, forcing him to lay on the bed. They spent the next ten minutes kissing, the following twenty minutes taking their clothes off piece by piece, and endless minutes exploring each other's bodies.

Richard was in good shape, but not all muscle and sinew which made her feel better about her jiggly bits.

They lay there breathless and wanting, but not moving forward as if the actual act would change the beauty in what they'd experienced so far.

"I say we go for it," she said. "And anything we mess up, we improve on the next round."

He rolled over and raised his body above hers. The minute he entered her was heaven. She'd only had sex in the back seat of a Dodge Ram Charger with a boy she thought she loved, but that wasn't love. Love was stronger and deeper and more complete; this was love and she felt it all the way to her bones.

In that moment, everything faded away and only he existed in her world. She was certain he felt the same because, as he moved with her, he looked at her like she was the last woman on earth.

She was right, it didn't take them long to find their pleasure. As they lay in bed folded around one another, she dared to dream of a future with a man who would always think she was enough.

CHAPTER TWENTY-SIX

One Month Later

"AVERY, HONEY, ARE YOU ALMOST READY?"

He tapped his shoe on the entry floor. They'd moved into their place a week ago but spent little time there. It wasn't as warm and homey as Courtney and Jesse's house, but she promised to help him make it feel like home. Nothing felt like home unless he was in her arms.

"I'm coming. I couldn't find my tennis shoes." She ran from her bedroom and stopped at the kitchen table to get Jesse's birthday present.

He looked around his new house and shook his head. Everything there needed to go. Moving all his modern furniture into a cabin was like putting fur on a fish and calling it a dog. It didn't make sense, but then, nothing made sense lately.

He had been convinced he was a loner and would never love again, and then he met Courtney, and everything changed. He still didn't have a job, but he had an opportunity. Tonight, he would run it past Courtney. They were a team, and as part of a team, all major decisions were up for discussion and a vote.

Hand in hand, they walked two houses down. In Avery's hand was Jesse's birthday present. The kids had moved past checkers and were diving into backgammon and that's what they got him.

He lifted his hand to knock. It was a habit even though no one expected him to. The door flew open, and Jesse welcomed them with a smile and a loud voice announcing that they were making a new Layer of Love cake but couldn't put the layers together until they arrived.

He turned and raced back to the kitchen while he and Avery followed.

When they got there, Courtney was standing by the island hugging the special occasion plate with one arm and holding a permanent marker with the other.

"Jesse and I want you to sign the plate."

His heart took off like a Learjet. The full and happy organ pounded heavily in his chest. This was Courtney's way of telling him they were at layer five.

"You know, that's permanent." He pointed to the pen.

She nodded. "Yes, that's the idea."

He closed the distance between them and hugged her with the plate pressing between them.

"If we sign that plate, you're never getting rid of us."

She grinned. "I know."

"Are you asking me to marry you?"

She gasped and stepped back. "No ... I mean..." She tilted her head and then stared at him. "What if I were, would you say yes?"

"Depends."

Her mouth dropped open. "What do you mean, depends?"

He took the plate and uncapped the lid. "If I sign this that means we're partners in everything."

"Okay."

He nodded to the chairs. "Have a seat, kids, this is our first family meeting."

Jesse rolled his eyes. "We always have meetings."

"This is different because the minute Avery and I sign this plate, everything changes."

Jesse shook his head. "I don't want things to change. I like it all the way it is."

"I get that, but what if this meeting meant things would be the same only better?"

"I'm listening," Jesse said.

Richard pulled a chair up for Courtney, kissed her head, and then stood beside her. The plate was still in his hand, as was the pen.

"How would you feel if I married your mom and called you my son?"

Jesse grinned. "I could live with that."

He turned to Avery. "What if you had Courtney as a mom. Would you like that?"

His daughter's cheeks pinked, and she nodded. "I love Courtney ... I mean Mom."

He set the plate on the counter along with the pen and moved to stand in front of Courtney.

"As for you, what would you think of becoming Mrs. Shipton and helping me run Altitude Flight School?"

"You bought the flight school?"

"I'm considering it, but I need to talk to my partner about it."

She cocked her head. "Are you asking me to marry you?"

He chuckled. "Yes, what do you say?"

She tapped her chin. "That depends."

He lifted a brow. "You have conditions?"

She picked up the plate and pen and handed it to Avery. "Sign it, sweetheart." Then she looked at Richard. "You want a wife and a bookkeeper?"

"I haven't put labels on everything. Ultimately, all I want is this." He pointed to all of them. "I want my family. You are mine. All of you."

She held his hand. "Will we have medical and dental insurance?" She looked at Avery. "Our daughter is going to need some mighty expensive implants down the road."

He laughed. "I'll get you the best insurance money can buy."

Jesse raised his hand. "I have some demands too."

"What would you like?"

He smiled. "I want to be a Shipton too, and I want a brother."

"I'll work on both."

He turned to Avery. "I know … you want a sister."

She nodded and smiled. "And a pony."

Courtney laughed. "We're going to need a different house— one with a barn."

Richard took the pen and signed the back of the plate. He and his family started building their love one layer at a time.

CHAPTER TWENTY-SEVEN

Three Months Later

"ARE YOU READY?" Richard asked.

"I need a minute." Courtney folded the paper and placed it into the pocket at the back of the book.

They'd spent most of the morning figuring out what they wanted to say as a family.

She closed the book and hugged it to her chest. If she had her way, she'd keep the book and make every single recipe in it, but rules were rules, and she didn't want to test fate.

She had everything she dreamed of and more.

"Kids, let's go," she called out, but no one answered.

"They're already outside." He leaned down and kissed her. "Are you ready for our first day?" The purchase of Altitude Flight School was complete, and this was their first day running it as a team.

"I'm so excited." She'd quit the bakery to become Richard's

full-time assistant. She'd run the books and the schedule, while he did all the flying.

He was as good as his word and bought the best health and dental plan he could afford.

She walked out of the house and to the SUV. Just as she got there, Avery dropped her backpack, and everything spilled out.

Putting the book on the roof of the car, she bent over to help her clean things up.

In went the math book, the pencils, and her lunch money.

"Here you go kiddo. You're good now." She kissed Avery on the head and told her she loved her. How could she not? She was the daughter she never knew she wanted, but now that she had her, she couldn't live without her.

She looked at her watch. "We need to go. Your dad has his first flight at nine."

The kids climbed into the car, and she took the front passenger seat.

Richard put the car into gear and backed out of the driveway. They dropped the kids off at school and were on their way when she realized she'd left the book on the roof of the SUV.

"Stop!"

Richard hit the brakes and then pulled off to the side of the road.

"What's wrong?"

She unbuckled her seatbelt and climbed out, frantically searching for the book, but it was gone.

"Oh no." Her hand went to her heart. "I left the book on the roof, and it's gone." A tear fell down her cheek. "What's going to happen now?"

He rounded the SUV and tugged her into his arms. "It's okay, sweetheart. Let me tell you what will happen. I'm going to love you forever, and *Recipes for Love* will find a new owner."

A LAYER OF LOVE CAKE RECIPE

Cake:

- 2¼ cups all-purpose flour (a binder, like honesty and faithfulness)
- 2 teaspoons baking powder (lifts like a bright smile on a dull day)
- ½ teaspoon salt (added to give life its flavor)
- ½ cup (1 stick) butter or margarine, softened (life's guilty pleasure)
- 1⅓ cups granulated sugar (this brings out our inner sweetness)
- 1 teaspoon vanilla extract (Get the good stuff, it's worth it.)
- ¾ cup milk (Use whole milk, this isn't a diet dessert.)
- 4 egg whites
- Icing colors as desired

ICING:

- ¾ cup solid vegetable shortening
- ¾ cup (1-1/2 sticks butter), or margarine, softened
- 1 ½ teaspoons vanilla extract
- 6 cups (about 1 ½ lbs.) sifted confectioners' sugar
- 2 to 3 tablespoons milk

DÉCOR

- Gather the edible sprinkles and glitter—this is your cake, and you like what you like.

PREHEAT OVEN to 325°F. Prepare 8-inch cake pans with vegetable spray.

IN A MEDIUM BOWL, sift together flour, baking powder and salt; set aside. In large bowl, beat butter and sugar with electric mixer until light and fluffy. Add egg whites one at a time, beating well after each addition. Add vanilla and beat well. Add flour mixture to butter mixture alternately with milk; beat until just combined.

DIVIDE BATTER evenly into 5 bowls (about ¾ cup batter in each bowl). Tint cake batter with icing colors to desired coloration.

Pour each bowl of batter into a prepared pan, scraping the sides as you pour.

BAKE 17 TO 20 MINUTES, rotating pans halfway between baking. Cakes are done when toothpick inserted in center comes out clean. Cool 5 minutes on cooling grid; remove from pans and cool completely before icing.

FOR ICING: Beat shortening and butter in large bowl with electric mixer until light and fluffy. Beat in vanilla. Gradually add sugar, one cup at a time, beating well on medium speed. Scrape sides and bottom of bowl often. When all sugar has been mixed in, icing will appear dry. Gradually add milk; beat at medium speed until light and fluffy.

TO ASSEMBLE: Place first layer on cake plate. Take your time as each layer builds on the next. Spread a layer of icing to edges of cake. Top with second cake. Repeat with remaining icing and cake layers. To finish, ice top and sides of cake and pretty it up.

IF CHOCOLATE IS what you're after, you can add ¼ cup of cocoa to the mix. This is your cake ... your way.

GET A FREE BOOK.

Go to www.authorkellycollins.com

SHOUTOUTS!

I wanted to give a big shoutout and thank you to my ARC team. Without them, this book would have been less.

Ann Jackson
Beth Waters Cotter
Carolyn Boyer
Deb Citron Mackow
Diana MacQuen
Donna Wolz
Ellen Creamer Hawrylciw
Jill Eshenbaugh
Katy Battisti
LaGina Keisha Hagerman-Reese
Marie Craig
Marlene Larsen
Mary Marsillett
Rose Cotton
Sabrina Medina
Sue Krainik

OTHER BOOKS BY KELLY COLLINS

Recipes for Love

A Tablespoon of Temptation

A Pinch of Passion

A Dash of Desire

A Cup of Compassion

A Dollop of Delight

A Layer of Love

The Second Chance Series

Set Free

Set Aside

Set in Stone

Set Up

Set on You

The Second Chance Series Box Set

ABOUT THE AUTHOR

International bestselling author of more than thirty novels, Kelly Collins writes with the intention of keeping love alive. Always a romantic, she blends real-life events with her vivid imagination to create characters and stories that lovers of contemporary romance, new adult, and romantic suspense will return to again and again.

For More Information
www.authorkellycollins.com
kelly@authorkellycollins.com

CPSIA information can be obtained
at www.ICGtesting.com
Printed in the USA
BVHW050208090223
658191BV00031B/1083